François Baron de Tott

Memories of the Baron de Tott

Vol. I

François Baron de Tott

Memories of the Baron de Tott
Vol. I

ISBN/EAN: 9783743387065

Manufactured in Europe, USA, Canada, Australia, Japa

Cover: Foto ©Andreas Hilbeck / pixelio.de

Manufactured and distributed by brebook publishing software (www.brebook.com)

François Baron de Tott

Memories of the Baron de Tott

MEMOIRS

OF THE

ᴅARON DE TOTT,

ON THE

TURKS AND THE TARTARS.

TRANSLATED FROM THE FRENCH,

BY AN ENGLISH GENTLEMAN AT PARIS,

UNDER THE IMMEDIATE INSPECTION OF

THE BARON.

———————

IN THREE VOLUMES.

VOL. I.

———————

DUBLIN:

PRINTED FOR L. WHITE, J. CASH, AND
R. MARCHBANK.
M,DCC,LXXXV.

PREFACE

TRANSLATOR

THE Tranſlator of the preſent work is ſenſible that he could not have taken a more diſadvantageous, or more ungrateful ſtation in the literary world. No merit in the tranſlation of living languages, can flatter the perſon who undertakes it, with the hopes of obtaining an adequate recompence for his labours, either in point of intereſt, or ambition ; yet the utility of his occupation is univerſally admitted, and

A 2   they

they who are acquainted with the two languages, muſt acknowledge, becauſe they
know, the difficulties he has to ſurmount,
to render a tranſlation tolerable.

To the deciſion of ſuch judges, the Tan-
ſlator ſubmits a work, he was induced to
attempt, from motives of utility, and with
the view of reſcuing an author of great merit, and authenticity, from ſuch treatment
as he had reaſon to apprehend from the
multitude of inaccurate and mutilated tran-
ſlations from the French, with which the
Engliſh preſs is daily teeming. Every
Raynal has not the good fortune to fall into the hands of a *Juſtamond.* He will only
add, on the ſubject of tranſlation, that it
were to be wiſhed, for the facility of that
literary commerce which is increaſing rapidly between the two firſt nations in Europe, *tam Marti, quam Mercurio,* that a Dictionary might be formed of all the ſynoni-
mous terms in Arts, Sciences, Natural Hiſtory, &c. in the two languages, the preſent
Dictionaries being ſo completely inadequate
to the purpoſes of tranſlation, in any of
thoſe branches. The extenſive and minute
knowledge

knowledge of the Baron de Tott, whilst it
astonishes the reader, in the course of these
Memoirs, will evince the utility, and, the
Translator fears, the necessity of this remark. It is certain, however, that in works
entirely devoted to arts and sciences, the
very best Translator, without such aid, will
find himself involved in insurmountable difficulties, which must necessarily lead to obscurity and confusion. The disuse of Latin
in the present age, as the medium of scien-
tific communication throughout Europe,
renders such a Dictionary particularly necessary for the two rival nations.

With respect to the original work, the
Translator thinks he may venture to pronounce, with some degree of confidence,
that these *Memoirs* will be at all times justly
held in estimation ; that they will furnish
entertainment and instruction for the man
of the world, and matter of profound meditation for the philosopher and politician.
Did they stand in need of any other recommendation than their own intrinsic merit,
the illustrious names of a *Choifeul* and a
Vergennes, stand as an unquestionable pledge
of

of the abilities and reputation of the ingenious and diftinguifhed author, whilft the
importance and varied objects of his feveràl
miflions, render all his remarks peculiarly
interefling.

A public ftation at the Ottoman Porte,
and amongft the Tartars, under fuch Minifters of a great, as well as the moft fa-
voured nation in that part of the world ; a
nation at all times celebrated too for its
difcernment and choice of able civil officers
and negociators ; a moft cultivated underftanding and comprehenfive knowledge,——
a thorough acquaintance with the language
and manners of the Turkifh empire, for
three and twenty years, the peculiar circumftances of the times wherein his abilities
were called into exertion, the fubfequent,
and future probable events, which bid fair,
perhaps in our days, to unhinge the whole
fyftem of European politics: thefe are
ftrong, unequivocal recommendations,
which fall to the lot of but few authors.

*Ricault, Marfigli, Lady Mary Wortley
Montague,* and *Sir James Porter,* have written

ten on the Turkish empire ; the two former
possess but a small degree of reputation ;
the second indeed very honestly sums up his
account by declaring, that it is almost im-
possible to form any judgment of that people. Our elegant countrywoman, with a
most voluptuous and animated pencil, has
transported her reader into the paradise of
Mahomet, by her lively powers of imagination ; has entered into competition with
the Prophet himself, and endeavoured to
convert our Christian men and women too,
into true believers. Sir James Porter alone
has the merit of having first given to the
world, true details, and accurate observations, on the manners of the Turks, founded
on facts, he was himself a witness to ; and
to which, these Memoirs bear honourable
testimony. As for the general class of travellers, their attention seems to have been
limited, to the barbarous nomenclature, of
the different officers of the Porte, without
explaining the true nature, and extent of
their employments, and by endeavouring
to assimilate them with those of our European Courts, where, in fact, there is no re-
semblance, to give the reader, the *Red Book*

of

of the Grand Signior, as a fubftitute for
every other fpecies of information, and leave
him bewildered in intricacies and errors.
As an hiftory, the annals of *Prince Cante-
mir*, deferve an honourable mention, and
are well worthy of perufal, as involving in
them, the true character of the Turkifh nation, and the influence of their government, from whence arofe thofe various revolutions, of which he is the hiftorian; but
never have this extraordinary government
and people been fo fully, or fo accurately
developed, as by the author of thefe Memoirs: divefted of prejudice too, and almoft fuperior to the reftraints of the country in which he writes, in painting the Ottoman empire, he has laid open errors and
crimes common to all defpotic governments,
and by boldly tracing them to defpotifm itfelf, has indirectly, but effectually ftood
forth, the champion of humanity. A citi-
zen himfelf, of a government, arbitrary,
at leaft in its principles, he has ventured to
hold out a terrible and falutary warning to
all nations, not quite fo far gone in flavery,
as the wretched orientals, to guard well their

few

few remaining rights, and to tremble for the total lofs of freedom.

After making the reader perfectly acquainted with the manners and monftrous government of the Turks, and correcting numberlefs errors of preceding travellers, can any thing be more curious or intereft-ing, than to fee this unweildy mafs in motion, and an empire confifting of eighty millions of inhabitants, poffeffed of the fineft climates and countries on the globe, upheld, and poffibly preferved, in a moft critical moment of its exiftence, by the fu-perior addrefs and underftanding of one fingle European?——All Europe knew, at the time, that the defence of the Darda-nelles againft the Ruffian fleet was intruft-ed to Mr. de Tott*, but never until the

A 5   publi-

* The judicious editor of the Annual Regifter, publifhed by Dodfley, in fpeaking of the campaigns between the Turks and Ruffians of 1773 and 1774, makes the following obfervations. " No details are " to be expected from a Turkifh Cabinet, or army; " and the Ruffians, fatisfied with their fuccefs, have " no occafion to enter into a recital of particulars, " which might leffen the glory or difficulty of their " atchieve-

publication of thefe Memoirs, was the world acquainted with the real weaknefs of that important paffage, the facility of forcing it, or the fingular exertions of its diftinguifhed defender. His labours, his firmnefs, and perfeverance, in overcoming every obftacle, in braving the moft inveterate prejudices, in conquering, and fubmitting to his will, the ftupid pride, the fanaticifm,

" atchievements. Such information can only be obtained near the fcene of action, and will " undoubtedly be hereafter communicated," either by " fome one of the moft curious and intelligent of the " European Minifters at the Porte, or of thofe foreign officers who ferved on the Danube. For " fuch curious and ufeful inquiries or details, we " have been more indebted to the induftry of the " French Minifters and Secretaries, for above a century paft, than to thofe of all the other nations in " Europe."—And in another place, " As the Turks " give no detail of their military tranfactions, and " the Ruffians only fuch a one as is fuited to the me- " ridian of their own people, no regular account is " to be expected, until fome future Manftein, among " their foreign officers, fhall get free from the " fhackles of power, and give an account of things " as they really are." As far as the circumftances admit, the reader will draw the parallel, and make the application.

the

the obstinacy, the jealousy, of this infatuated people; and, above all, their contempt and hatred of the Christians.—The unalterable confidence reposed in him by the Grand Signior, justified by the most astonishing success in this defence, as well as in his subsequent proceedings, form, altogether, a series of particulars unexampled in history. By the force of his own genius, aided only by the *Memoirs of Saint Remy*, and the *Encyclopedia*, Mr. de Tott learnt himself, and taught his dangerous pupils to cast and bore cannon, to employ their artillery, and to make pontoons. He changed their arms, their evolutions, their discipline, their principles of ship-building, and fortification; he founded different schools, and was himself at once the mechanical workman, and the guide and inventor of these various reforms.

His account of the Tartars would at all times have been extremely curious, but is more particularly so at this moment, as it is perhaps the last glance we shall have of that ancient and interesting people, as a distinct and independent nation. Russia is

now

now in complete poſſeſſion of the Crimea, from whence ſhe is already making naval armaments; and from the rapid progreſs made in one century, in arts and arms, by that vaſt empire, it may be conjectured, without any extraordinary ſtretch of imagination, that the beautiful and happy ſituation, and immenſe population of the Tauric Cherſoneſus, will prove in her hands, the ſource and inſtrument of conſiderable, and perhaps, not very diſtant revolutions. In this part of the Memoirs, there is a rich feaſt for the philoſopher and politician.— They will here find, amongſt an infinite variety of new and intereſting materials, a number of European cuſtoms, which certainly have not travelled eaſtward, our ancient feudal ſyſtem, and a pretty correct model of Engliſh legiſlature, with an improvement on the democratical part of that celebrated inſtitution, revived by the people of America, in ſeveral of their new conſtitutions; I mean, the inſuring to the people the meeting of the deliberative branch of the legiſlature, independent of the executive power; as we ſee that the Bey of the Chirins, in the Tartar conſtitution,

could

could convoke the aſſembly of the other
Beys, even if the Kam, like Charles the Firſt,
ſhould be diſpoſed to diſpenſe with this
neceſſary controul. Thus has modern fore-
ſight ſupplied, what has probably been loſt
in the deſcent from the original authors of
this, as well as other uſages of the northern
nations.

Notwithſtanding our author has been
obliged to tread over beaten ground in the
latter part of the third volume, the reader
will find it replete with new and ingenious
remarks and diſcuſſions; and as a commercial nation, England cannot with an indifferent eye, view her rivals in poſſeſſion of
the whole commerce of the Levant, nor
the unremitted attention ſhe continues to
beſtow on this important ſource of her
wealth and proſperity. Happy too, if ſhe
could be prevailed on to take a leſſon from
the political conduct of her powerful and
riſing neighbour. She would not then
continue to hazard her intereſts, and leſſen
her conſequence in the eyes of Europe, by
ſending a Ch——d to repreſent her policy
at the Court of one of the firſt branches of
the

the House of Bourbon, whilst she has the example of France, deputing a De Tott, to reside with the Kam of the Tartars, and to negociate with the Confederates of Poland *.

The Translator has taken the liberty of pronouncing with much confidence on the fidelity of these Memoirs, if it were possible to entertain a doubt, from the circumstance of his being honoured with the personal acquaintance of the Baron de Tott †,

and

* It is a certain fact, although not generally known, that the Duke de Choiseul, the same Minister who sent M. de Tott on his mission to the Tartars, employed the Baron de Kaalb, in the year 1765, soon after the laying of the fatal Stamp Act, to sound the dispositions, and tamper with the American leaders. The same Baron de Kaalb remained twelve months in that country, and until the wise measure of the repeal, by the Rockingham administration. He returned to America, however, at the commencement of hostilities, and lost his life fighting under General Gates, at the memorable battle of Camden.

† The chagrin of the Court of Russia on being made acquainted with the state of the defence, when their fleet was off the Dardanelles, must be very great.

M. de

and the opportunities he has had of, converfing with Mr. Rufin.*, a man of the
ftricteft

M. de Tott informed the Tranflator, that after the
conclufion of the peace, he met with Prince Repnin,
whom he had formerly known at Warfaw, on his arrival in quality of Ruffian Ambaffador at Conftantinople : dining together, with the other foreign Minifters, at le Comte de St. Prieft's, the Prince was congratulated on the return of peace, and his appearance
at the Porte; on which, turning to M. de St. Prieft,
with a farcaftic air, he faid, " We fhould have arrived here much fooner, if M. de Tott would have permitted us." The time and place, which fhould have
precluded the remark, permitted M. de Tott only to
reply, " Your Excellency does me too much honour;
I do affure you that I only went to the Dardanelles to
fee your fleet pafs." The Ambaffador foon had the
mortification to afcertain the truth on which this re-
partée was founded.

    * Mr. Rufin was made a prifoner by the Ruffians
in a, fecond inroad of the Tartars, under Dewlet-
Gueray, fucceffor to Krim-Gueray; and after being
deprived of all his-papers, was kept confined twelve
months, under pretence of his not being a Frenchman, although he was known to be Chargé d'Affaires,
after the departure of the Baron de Tott.—A Ruffian
officer reproaching him one day with having directed
the artillery of Kotchim for the Turks, Mr. Rufin
afked him what execution it had done in the Ruffian
camp? " We had one man, and four horfes killed,"
replied the Ruffian.—" I leave you to judge, then,"
says

ſtricteſt veracity, and the moſt correct un-
derſtanding, who was Secretary Interpreter
to the Baron, when amongſt the Tartars,
and has lived alſo in Turkey; and from his
intimacy

ſays Mr. Rufin, whether the cannon were pointed by
a Frenchman."

A noble inſtance of female tenderneſs and Turkiſh
cruelty, which the Tranſlator had from Mr. Rufin,
deſerves to be recorded.—In the firſt inroad into New
Servia by Krim Gueray, the account of which is
given in theſe Memoirs, the Kam, anxious, as far as
he was able, to alleviate the horrors of that ſpecies of
war to which the Tartars are accuſtomed, and deſirous, as we have ſeen, of preſerving the Poliſh territory from violation, appointed inſpectors to viſit all
the waggons, and tents, and gave orders for all the
perſons who were taken for the purpoſe of carrying
them into ſlavery, to be brought for examination to
theſe inſpectors. One of thoſe barbarous Turkiſh
Sipahis, ſo well characterized by Mr. de Tott, came
riding up to Mr. Rufin, in conſequence of this regulation, and demanded, if he was one of the perſons
appointed to receive the ſlaves? Mr. Rufin ſeeing
him with four infants in his arms, and, to uſe his
own expreſſion, when ſpeaking of it to the Tranſlator,
which he could compare to nothing but a birds neſt
this ruffian had juſt been robbing, humanely anſwered
in the affirmative; the barbarian cried out, " Take
them," and throwing them with violence from his
horſe,

intimacy with Mr. Du Rocher, a gentleman of the moft amiable manners, and
great honour, who has long faithfully
ferved his Court, as Conful at Tripoli, and
Tunis, underftands perfectly the Turkifh
language, has travelled through Egypt, and
other parts of the Ottoman dominions, and
is well acquainted with the cuftoms and
manners of Conftantinople.

It is with concern that the Tranflator
has obferved in *Dodfley's Annual Regifter* for
1773, a work of great and merited reputation, and which will certainly furnifh
the beft materials for future hiftorians, an
account of the Baron de Tott, equally un-
true and injurious to his honour and reputation. The paffage is founded on a mif-

horfe, rode off full gallop. The ground was fortunately covered with fnow, that the poor infants received no hurt. Mr. Rufin was embarraffed, no
doubt, with this prefent, but not difcouraged from
the duties of humanity; with much difficulty he found
the parents of three of them, and the fourth was taken
by a poor woman, who was fufficiently encumbered
with children of her own, but having formerly loft
an infant in the fame way, chearfully embraced and
adopted the loft innocent.

take,

take, pardonable, 'tis true, from the obfcurity of the narratives of the day, and
the extreme difficulty ſtated by the Editor,
of aſcertaining facts, in the war between
the Turks and Ruſſians, but which the
Tranſlator has no doubt but he will readily
embrace the opportunity of correcting,
from his known candour, and love of
truth, in the next volume of his moſt uſe-
ful hiſtory. The Baron, indeed, is not
named, but the alluſion is too pointed to
admit of doubt ; beſides that, his name is
mentioned in the volume for 1774, page 6.
of the *Hiſtorical Part*, in his account of
the victory gained over the Reis Effendi,
on the 20th of June, wherein the fine
train of artillery taken by the Ruſſians, is
truly ſaid to have been " caſt under the
directions of the *Chevalier de Tott.*" The
paſſage is as follows :—" *A French Rene-*
" *gado*, who had been the Conſul to that
" nation at the Dardanelles, and had
" baſely fixed the ſtigma upon his coun-
" try, of producing the firſt public officer
" belonging to any Weſtern State, who
" had abandoned Chriſtianity, to embrace
" Mahometaniſm, formed a kind of mili-
" tary

" tary fchool, under the fanction and im-
" mediate infpection of the Grand Signior,
" which in the prefent difpofition of the
" Turks, may be productive of fome ef-
" fect. This man, having a competent
" degree of mathematical knowledge, and
" being well verfed in the management of
" artillery, had been employed, *prior to*
" *his apoftacy*, in repairing the caftles, and
" erecting new fortifications at the Dar-
" danelles; fo that, independent of the
" defence of a fleet, that paffage might,
" from its own ftrength, be rendered im-
" practicable to the Ruffians. That fer-
" vice having been performed to the fatis-
" faction of the Porte, and *this adventurer*
" *being now become its fubject*, he under-
" took the inftruction of the Turkifh en-
" gineers, and attended to this office with
" fuch affiduity, that, it is faid, he has
" already accomplifhed a furprizing im-
" provement in the management of their
" artillery."

The fact is, that the Baron de Tott never was Conful at the Dardanelles; but the
Vice-Confulfhip, *a poft of no fort of confe-*
quence,

quence, was then held by a very low perfon, of the name of Guys; who appre-
hending the refentment of the French
Ambaffador, for fome offence he had committed, bafely affumed the turban; and
was, in confequence, thoroughly defpifed,
as all renegadoes are by the Turks, as well
as his own countrymen *. The reft of
this

---

* Mr. de Tott has ftated to the tranflator the
impracticability of the Turks receiving any effential
permanent inftructions from the Europeans, on this
very principle, viz. that the inftant their inftructor
becomes a Mahometan, he is looked upon as a fellow fubject, and is reduced to a level with themfelves, befides the contempt naturally attending a
forced converfion; and if he remains a Chriftian, he
has infuperable obftacles to overcome, even with the
unufual and improbable protection and firmnefs of a
Sultan Muftapha. Amongft others, the famous Mr.
De Bonneval, whofe hiftory made fo much noife at
the beginning of this century, may be rated as an
example of the truth of this obfervation. No Chriftian can ever be more refpectably fituated than Mr.
De Tott, yet even his regulations produced only a
momentary effect, and are already fallen into decay.
On this fubject, it may not be improper to add the
two following anecdotes:—

One of the beft officers of the King of Pruffia,
tempted by various reports in the European Gazettes,
of the lucrative and advantageous fituations to be
obtained

this man's history, which the Translator
had from the Baron de Tott, and Mr. du
Rocher, is not worth relating. The Baron,
indeed, laughed at the passage when it was
shown

obtained at the Porte, without any trouble, by an
officer of merit, set out for Constantinople with the
best possible certificates, the testimonial of that great
Captain his royal master. On his arrival he presented himself to the Envoy, communicating to him
his intentions of disciplining, and commanding the
Turkish troops. The Envoy endeavoured to con-
vince him of his error, and to dissuade him from his
project, assuring him that his services could not be
accepted. " What," says the officer, " is not Mr.
De Tott, at this very hour, employed and making
a fortune under them." " Let us wait on that gentleman," replies the Envoy, " since you will not be
convinced by me, and you will then hear his account
of the matter." They called on the Baron, who confirmed the Envoy's observations, by the most striking
facts, assuring him, amongst other circumstances,
that he had never received a farthing from the Porte,
nor any other appointment than that of his own
Court. Still he is not satisfied.—He addresses himself directly to the Porte, and obtains an audience of
the Reis Effendi, who after listening to all his recommendations, very coolly answered him: " all
this is very well, but there is one little requisite you
seem to have forgot." " What is that ?" demanded
the officer ;—" only the trifling ceremony of becoming a Mahometan." The officer with great
warmth

fhown him ; but on the Tranflator's reprefenting to him the work, with the refpect
it merits, he was not fo indifferent to ho-
neft fame, as not to wifh to call upon the
juftice

warmth cites Mr. De Tott, as a proof that a Chriftian may be employed. " Aye," fays the Minifter,
" that is very true, and appears to us all very aftonifh-
ing; but that is no fort of rule,—the Grand Signior
choofes it fhould be fo, and we muft obey him ; but
I tell you once more, that it is an example, which
will not be repeated—Mr. De Tott's is a very extraordinary cafe." It is unneceffary to add, that the officer was not employed.

The other anecdote is of the Swedifh Envoy, who
zealoufly interefted himfelf at all times, in favour of
Mr. De Tott's regulations. Converfing one day
with one of the firft Minifters of the Porte, on that
fubject, he afked him, whether he had not made
great improvements ? " Yes," replies the Minifter,
" but"—" But what," fays the Envoy, giving fome
recent inftance of his fkill, " is not that furprifing ?"
" Yes truly," refumed the Minifter drily, " but
what is ftill more furprifing, is, that he is ftill alive."
The Envoy flew to Mr. De Tott, related the converfation, and the manner in which this was faid,
conjuring him to be on his guard ; and above all not
to drink coffee with them when he waited on the Minifters. Mr. De Tott thanked him for his fears, but
obferved, that his fafety lay in the terrors of the Minifters themfelves, and the favour and protection of
the Grand Signior, adding, that if they dared to attempt

juftice of the Editor, that his honour may
be vindicated to the Englifh nation, and
to Europe, through the fame refpeclable
channel by which it has been unintention-
ally wounded. The Tranflator, therefore,
in his name, and for the credit of the
work itfelf, lays claim to juftice in that
particular, leaving " the competency of
the Baron's mathematical knowledge,"
and other qualifications, to be determined by the judgment of the readers of
thefe Memoirs. However he may value
his fcientific reputation, nothing is fo dear
to the Baron de Tott as his perfonal honour *.

PARIS,
March 16, 1785.

tempt his life, no precaution he could take, would
infure it, befides that betraying fuch an apprehenfion,
was the moft probable means of fuggefting the idea.

* Mr. De Tott is in poffeffion of a curious *French
poem*, from the *Royal Prefs at Mofcow*, wherein a-
mongft a variety of *barbarous* epithets, in *barbarous*
verfe, he is alfo portrayed as a purchafed renegado.
How frail is fame, and how ineffectual the exertions
of an active and ufeful life, when we confider that
hiftory is not unfrequently obliged to decorate her
dignity, with the vileft trappings!!

PRELIMINARY DISCOURSE.

HISTORY appears, at the firft glance, to prefent us with nothing but a fcene of horror, where the victims are brought upon the ftage, only to throw a luftre on thofe executioners of mankind, who facrifice them to their paffions, but it lays before us at the fame time the valuable defcription of manners; and that part of Hiftory will appear undoubtedly the moft interefting, when we confider that a nation is governed by its ancient cuftoms, as the conduct of an individual is guided by his perfonal character. From what more fertile fource can we derive a perfect knowledge of mankind, or learn to govern them?

In this point of view, Hiftory ought to form a moft interefting object of attention in the policy of all governments: it will there be feen, that cuftoms, by creating and modifying, infenfibly, their manners, form, in every part of the world, the great fpring by which mankind are put in motion. Cuftoms lay the foundation of, and

produce

produce the great Revolutions of Empires;
they form the ftructure, and either enfure
its ftability, or undermine it by degrees;
and are the caufes of its total deftruction.
The flownefs of the approach conceals the
progrefs of the evil; and its fatal advances
are unperceived until the moment when
he, who could apply the remedy, receives
himfelf a ftroke he is unable to repel without that force of which he is no longer
mafter.

If we leave in obfcurity thofe torrents of
robbers, who, in ravaging the earth, have
trampled under foot thofe fmall focieties
which affumed the pompous title of Empires; if we except too fome petty ftates,
who, after increafing the population of infant Rome, carried the reputation of her
arms fo far as to procure the fubmiffion of
feveral countries by the fimple fummons of
her heralds, no powerful nation has ever
really fallen from the attack of a foreign
enemy; no empire, firmly eftablifhed, has
ever been overthrown by the fate of an unfortunate battle.   Greece, enflaved by the
Romans; Rome, herfelf, deftroyed by the
Barbarians, fell lefs a facrifice to foreign
force, than to her own internal weaknefs.

This

This truth has no need of examination : it is perhaps the only point which Hiftory, in treating of the rife and fall of ancient empires, has illuftrated completely. But why may not an inquiry into their reigning manners and cuftoms, ferve to elucidate the Hiftory of thofe people who have not even preferved any tradition of their own ? Their manners will be, with refpect to them, what the Parian marbles have been for the Greeks, but a monument undoubtedly of greater value. We have only to decypher the characters. The fpirit of each nation will ferve in the ftead of its ancient infcriptions; and we fhall there difcover the type of thofe great events which muft have happened in former ages. ——Thofe nations, whofe manners appear the moft refined, muft for that reafon have undergone more frequent revolutions; and we may conclude, that the people, who difcover in their manners only thofe effects which arife from the natural influence of climate, have never been fubdued. In fact, if we confider defpotifm as exercifed now under the torrid zone, and again towards the polar circle, is it poffible to attribute the manners of any nation to the

fole

fole influence of climate? If we fuppofe
that the republican principle was prior to
that of defpotifm, how can the latter have
totally obliterated every trace of ancient
liberty? Such revolutions, however, have
covered the furface of the globe, and appear to be the real caufe of that variety of
manners which fo far diftinguifh, at this
day, the refpective nations, as to occafion
a vifible alteration in the natural and primitive features of all human focieties. Bring
together a Manchou and a Bafs-Arabian
Tartar, you will fearch in vain the interval of fifteen hundred leagues that feparates their countries: the climate differs
but little; the government is the fame.
Then confider the Greek and the Turk,
whofe habitations touch; you will there
recover the fifteen hundred leagues that
you had loft; yet they live under the fame
fky, and under the fame conftitution. Let
the Arab, who, under the burning tropic,
goes to refrefh himfelf at the cataracts of
the Nile, take place of the Manchou, to
the north of China, he will there exhibit
more moral analogy with the Tartar than
he did with the Egyptians, his countrymen; but let him pafs the River Amur,
and

and he will form a ftriking contraft with the Ruffian foldier. And, in purfuing this inquiry, the influence of government will appear more diftinctly marked on the characters of individuals, than that of climate : we fhall perceive moral, conftantly prevailing over natural, caufes, and giving the folution of thofe various fhades of difference, which appear the moft difficult of explanation.

It is by confidering, in this point of view, the defcendants of Patroclus and Achilles, that one perceives that under the influence of the fame climate, the defpotifm that has crufhed the later Greeks, fubdued formerly by Alexander, although it has marked them with the character of flavery, has not been able to efface the outlines of that religious pufillanimity which overturned the empire of the Greeks. It is thus, that by remounting to the ancient period of Grecian glory, we fhall find in the principles of her early government, the correctives of that climate, which invites its inhabitants more to enjoy, than to be indifferent about life. The weaknefs of the lower empire could not fail to enervate thofe minds which had

been

been influenced in former times by the exalted motives of glory, liberty, and virtue; and it is under the yoke of the prefent tyrants, that natural caufes muft refume their empire. Thefe natural caufes muft neceffarily predominate, if not oppofed by moral obftacles; and defpotifm deftroys them. This government too has lefs influence than any other on the multitude which it oppreffes;—the principal inftruments of the oppreffion of the people, conftitute its main fpring and fupport.

If the climate which the Turks inhabit relaxes their fibres, the defpotifm under which they groan tranfports them to violence. They are not unfrequently ferocious;——their fyftem of predeftination adds to their fiercenefs; and the fame prejudice that in a cold climate would have rendered them courageous, in a hot one produces nothing but fanaticifm and rafhnefs *; the burning fever which elevates
their

---

* The Turks furnifh continual proofs of this affertion, in their quarrels with one another. Drunkennefs is the neceffary preparative for vengeance. Affaffination is the only method they employ; they face no danger in cold blood. An Ottoman army once
attacked,

their brain, makes them defpife every thing that is not Turkifh ; and from that mode of reafoning with themfelves, pride and ignorance are the natural refult.   It is for this reafon, that in the very cradle of the arts, in the country of Pericles, of Euclid, and of Homer, the fciences are fpoken of, at this day, only with a fneer of contempt.

But notwithftanding all men are attracted by renown, and are invariably put in motion by felf love, although their object be not immediately the fame ; and the Turks are perhaps the only men who have made choice of murder as the road to fame, without poffeffing energy of mind fufficient to commit it in cold blood. Whilft the climate difpofes to weaknefs on the one hand, and defpotifm urges to violence on

attacked, is broken to pieces without being beaten ; but the firft fhock of the Turks, when they are determined to make the firft attack, is always dangerous and difficult to fuftain. At the affair of Grotfka, to get poffeffion of a redoubt, they heaped the ditches with their dead ; and fanaticifm carried fome of them fo far in the laft war againft the Ruffians, as to make them brave the fire of the artillery by rufhing, like madmen, to hack with their fabres the mouths of the enemy's cannon.

the

the other, intoxication becomes neceſſary
to give them vigour ; and, to perpetrate a
crime with them, is to raiſe themſelves to
a level with their deſpot.

By reflecting on the connection between
the manners and cuſtoms of every nation,
its climate, and preſent form of government, and by obſerving with attention the
different traces of their antient governments, one cannot help beholding with
horror the thoughtleſs multitude always
leaning to the defective ſide, and invariably preſerving the inſtruments of their
own moral deſtruction.

Is it poſſible not to diſtinguiſh clearly
this effect on the moſt celebrated of all
people, at this day the laſt of nations, although it be even now the moſt numerous
and moſt univerſally diſperſed ? The Jews,
who cover the earth with their induſtry,
without having preſerved any legitimate
right of poſſeſſion, ſubmitting to the im-
pulſions of every government where they
are to be found, ſtill retain, in the midſt
of thoſe different governments, a ſhadow
of their ancient theocracy, in the exerciſe
of a kind of tolerated municipality; and
which alone is capable of feeding that
                                    ſtupid

ſtupid pride, that renders them inſenſible to inſult. The Jews carry this infenſibility even into cold and mountainous countries, where the human race, ſtrongly conſtituted, is always courageous, and often vindictive. Moral habits always prevail over natural cauſes, except when tyranny, or the abuſe of liberty, reſtores them to all their rights.

If, in order to weigh more minutely this laſt aſſertion, we undertake to confront the diſtinguiſhing characteriſtics of all nations, with their reſpective hiſtories, it will be neceſſary, no doubt, amidſt the croud of intereſting events, to draw a line between thoſe which have only tranſiently affected them, and ſuch as have been followed by the incorporation of the victors and the vanquiſhed. Torrents only ſweep before them the ſurface of the earth, without impairing the ſoil :—this diſtinction is eſſential, that we may not confound a madman who over-runs Aſia to ſubjugate the earth after having laid it waſte, with Alexander building Alexandria, to give a center to the univerſe, and to unite the two hemiſpheres of the globe. It is not leſs important to obſerve the nature of the

con-

conquered country, fo as to diftinguifh
the inhabitants of the mountains, who are
never thoroughly reduced, from thofe of
the plains, who are always eafily fubdued.
In this point of view, there is not even a
kingdom, there is not even a province,
where the people do not effentially differ,
although confounded under the fame deno-
mination. We fhall very eafily diftinguifh
too, amongft them, the different effects
even of the fame form of government ;
and this difference will eternally exift. Man
has an invincible tendency to liberty ; the
moment that he difcovers the poffibility of
enjoying, he determines to obtain it : in
a hilly country, he preferves an independence which the fituation favours ; accuftomed to climb the mountains, he traverfes
them with eafe, and it is from their fummit that he braves that power, to which
the inhabitant of the plain is as fubmiffive
from cuftom, as from the nature of the
country, and in which eafe and plenty con-
ciliates his fubjection ; whilft on the other
hand, the hardy mountaineer finds, in the
charm of liberty alone, an ample compenfation for the wants and fatigues infepar-
able from his fituation.

In

In travelling along the coaft of Syria, we fee defpotifm extending itfelf over all the flat country, and its progrefs ftopt towards the mountains, at the firft rock, at the firft defile, that is eafy of defence; whilft the Curdi, the Drufi, and the Mutuali, mafters of Libanon, and Anti-Libanon, conftantly preferve their independence, their manners, and the memory of the famous Facardin. The Macedonians formerly fubdued, could not eafily have been fo; but in their plains and their mountains muft have afforded them as fure an afylum againft the tyranny of the Romans, as they ftill furnifh them at this day againft the Ottoman yoke. No revolution therefore has impaired, among this hardy race, the influence of climate. From the days of the hero of Greece, without any intermediate epocha, indefatigable hufbandmen, and as brave as they are laborious, always united in defence of the common caufe; and each individual finding in himfelf refource fufficient to revenge a perfonal injury, they ftill chaunt the victories of Alexander, with the certainty of again obtaining frefh ones, over the firft enemy they encounter.

There

There is no nation on which fo much has been written as on the Turks; and no prejudices more readily believed than thofe which are adopted on the fubject of their manners. The voluptuoufnefs of the eaft-ern nations, the delirium of happinefs they enjoy, furrounded by many women, the beauty of thofe who people their pretended feraglios, their intrigues and gallantries, the courage of the Turks, the noblenefs of their actions, their generofity——what an accumulation of errors! even their juf-tice has been quoted as a model. But how is it poffible, fays Montefquieu, that the moft ignorant of all people can have feen clearly, in the circumftance in the world, which it behoves them the moft to under-ftand?

This objection could not efcape the eye of genius. Mr. de Montefquieu might have equally denied the Turks that deli-cate voluptuoufnefs, and the principles of that greatnefs of mind, and generofity, which they have been fuppofed to poffefs. He might have perceived that an unenlight-ened nation can contribute nothing to its own happinefs, becaufe its ignorance par-

takes

takes of a principle, which conftantly deftroys, without ever being productive.

An individual in France or England, if
he be rich, though ignorant, may there
enjoy a kind of happinefs which will flatter his imagination. His miftrefs fhall be
amiable ; he fhall even find feveral who
agree together ; his houfe fhall be elegantly
furnifhed ; he fhall be well dreffed, and
have a handfome equipage ; and the practice of borrowing the ideas of others, fhall
conceal even his ignorance. He is like an
opaque body in the midft of a great mafs
of light. In an enlightened nation, riches
procure every thing : to an ignorant people they are fo much the more a burthen,
as having no method of employing them,
they content themfelves with hoarding ;
men apply themfelves more eagerly to the
art of amaffing wealth, when the impof-
fibility of enjoying it leaves them only the
barren refource of accumulation.

But riches alone are not fufficient to procure a man the true enjoyment of his fortune. There are but few happy men in
the clafs of opulence, becaufe it is more
eafy to abufe, than to make a proper ufe of
riches. This is perhaps the only inftance
where

where ignorance adopts the fimpleft method; yet it cannot be denied, that knowledge is as neceffary to true enjoyment, as
temperance is to health.   If thefe reflections naturally occur to every man who can
and will reflect, how happens it that a
commercial intercourfe of two centuries
betwixt Europe and the Turks, fhould be
productive only of falfe notions refpecting
them; and why fhould the reader, who
really fearches after knowledge, beftow
more credit on the prefent, than on any
former narrative? What are my particular
claims to credibility?

But thefe are obfervations which never
occurred on the fubject of the pretended
letters of Lady Mary Wortley Montague.
They pleafed, and that was enough for the
author; and too often this is all the reader
looks for. The ftory of a Cady's head,
offered by a Janiffary to that Ambaffadrefs,
inftead of fome pigeons which fhe had defired, cannot fail of entertaining more than
an account of the death of the three favourites of the Sultan Mahomout *, whom
that

* Sultan Mahomout had beftowed all his confidence on Kiflar Aga, who, in his turn, trufted every
thing

that Prince was obliged to facrifice, to atone for an infult offered to another Cady.

In the former ftory the ridiculoufnefs of the circumftance is concealed by its gaiety, whilft the latter prefents nothing but an

thing to a young Turk of the name of Soliman, and he gave himfelf up entirely to Zacoub, an Armenian banker; this triumvirate ftudied every thing which could excite and contribute to the Sultan's pleafures, by which means thefe favourites gratified their rapacioufnefs, and confirmed their credit. They had the entire government of the empire, and every office was fold to the beft bidder; a whifper from them difpofed of the moft inconfiderable employment. Arrived at length, at that pitch of infolence which cannot bear the flighteft contradiction, one of their creatures had the boldnefs to threaten, with his whip, the Judge of Scutary, who raifed his voice and appealed to Juftice. His houfe was, in confequence, deftroyed in the night; but this method of filencing the complaint; produced fuch difcontents, that fome new fire broke out every day at Conftantinople. A fingular method of compelling the Sovereign's attention, but which was fo fuccefsful, as to determine the Grand Signor to order the heads of his favourites to be taken off, and as they had inftructed him in the habits of varying his pleafures, he affifted in perfon at the execution of the young Soliman, and of Zacoub; Kiflar Aga was executed in Leander's Tower.

example

example of the abuſes of deſpotiſm, and
the weakneſs of the deſpot, at which humanity ſhudders.

There is nothing ſo common when one
is unacquainted with the language, as to
adopt, and give falſe notions of the country where one travels; and that too, under a firm conviction that we are right,
and with a moſt earneſt deſire of being
minutely exact.   After reflecting on Lady
Montague's ſtory of her Janiſſary, her
Cady, and her pigeons, I think I have diſ-
covered in the genius of the Turkiſh language and people, the ſolution of her error,
notwithſtanding the literal tranſlation of
the Janiſſary's anſwer, ſuppoſed to be
given by her interpreter.   In fact, it is not
unlikely, that tired of ſearching for the
pigeons, which are leſs taken care of, and
more wild in Turkey, and rudely repulſed
by the Cady; out of humour, perhaps, at
the demands of the female traveller, he
may have taken upon him to aſk, " if he
ſhould bring the Cady's head?" And if,
in addition to this anſwer, we figure to
ourſelves an air and tone of impatience, it
will appear really to convey more contempt
for the Ambaſſadreſs than for the Judge;
and

and this is, probably, what the interpreter did not faithfully tranflate to Lady Mary Montague.

It is thus that travellers, deprived of the only means by which they can travel; to effect, have publifhed and given fanction to numberlefs abfurdities, without meriting any other reproach than that of not being fufficiently diffident of themfelves. I truft that this judgment will appear moderate and impartial.

One remark, however, I muft make, with refpect to thofe who put implicit confidence in that collection of reveries. To the reader who wifhes to be amufed with fuch idle dreams, my obfervation will be ufelefs. I addrefs myfelf to fuch only as are really in fearch of inftruction. How is it poffible to overlook the moft palpable contradictions ? Are there no certain rules for diftinguifhing the truth ? Will you believe, becaufe you are told fo, that a man with one arm has made ufe of both ; or that a man with one eye fees better by fhutting it ? If then you cannot give credit to fuch monftrous abfurdities, how can you be prevailed upon to imagine, tha thofe faculties which alone can make men happy,

are

are not totally deſtroyed by deſpotiſm?
Admit for a moment this monſter in politics, obſerve well the conſequences, follow
up the detail, combine its circumſtances,
and it will be impoſſible any longer to deceive you, except in a few details of no
importance, and the embelliſhments of the
author. This, however, is of itſelf ſufficient to eſtabliſh and perpetuate innumerable errors. I might myſelf have committed the ſame fault, had I, in writing of
the Turks, given way to thoſe ſentiments
with which they have inſpired me. It is
neceſſary not to decide partially, and to be
diffident even of one's own judgment.
With reſpect to myſelf, it is by living
amongſt them three and twenty years,
and under various circumſtances, that I
have obtained a knowledge of their character *. It is from the manner, therefore, in which I have viewed them, that I
have formed my opinions. To enable

---

* From the principles I have laid down on the neceſſity of knowing the language of any nation with
which one wiſhes to be thoroughly acquainted, it
cannot be ſuppoſed that I have neglected this moſt
eſſential method of obtaining a knowledge of the
Turks.

thoſe

thofe who really wifh for information to
judge for themfelves, I fhall furnifh them
with the fame materials, by giving a faith-
ful narrative of events, and placing
them in the fame point of view. The
impreffion the picture I am about to lay
before them made, on myfelf, is of little
importance.

This reflection has determined me to
write only a Journal of what paffed during
my refidence in Turkey, and in Tartary,
and a narrative of my laft voyage up the
Levant; and I fhall confine myfelf to fuch
obfervations as may be neceffary to elucidate the facts, without even venturing on
a detail of circumftances, to which I was
not myfelf a witnefs. To confent to be
ignorant, is an excellent method of obtaining knowledge; and when an Author
allows that he is fo, he puts in a ftrong
claim to the confidence of his reader. But
this is by no means the fyftem of thofe
travellers who are anxious to conduct their
readers into the inmoft receffes of the Seraglio, receffes abfolutely impenetrable.
To ftudy their manners, the influence of
their government and climate, and to examine their particular cuftoms, thefe are
the

the only means by which we can escalade the walls of the ancient Byzantium *. But of the various objects which merit our attention, amongst such a people as the Turks, is there none then so interesting as the history of their women? Of what consequence is it to mankind to be informed, that any individual, who from fortune and the prejudices of his country, has the free enjoyment of forty women, collects them together, and keeps them in a cage? In reading such a description, we can only lament the hard fate of this groupe of unhappy victims, and pronounce, without hesitation, that they are not very happy amongst themselves. But it is undoubtedly of some importance to study the effects of this extraordinary state of things, which is as far removed as possible from the state of nature. The slightest reflection will explain those effects, and an enquiry into their manners, will confirm the result.

Having, from my situation, had few opportunities of speaking of the Turkish

* The limits of the ancient Byzantium are at present entirely occupied by the Grand Signior's Seraglio.

women,

women, I have thought it neceffary to attempt to rectify the erroneous ideas which
prevail refpecting them, by making fome
remarks on the plurality of wives, their
manner of exifting in that melancholy fort
of fociety, and, in fliort, on the abufes
which arife from the very circumftance of
that affociation.

I fhall gratify at once my own impatience, and that of the public, by beginning
with the fubject ; but if they are anxious to
penetrate into the interior of the harems *,
they will very foon be as defirous as myfelf of getting out of them, to purfue, with
me, an enquiry more worthy their attention.

The Coran, which forms a code of civil
and criminal laws, as well as of morals and
religious worfhip, and which, with the
latitude of interpretation intrufted to the
Judges, provides for every contingercy,

* The word Harem, is ftrictly confined to fignify
the apartments of the women, the inclofure appropriated to their ufe : it muft never be confounded
with Seraglio, which means a Palace. All the
Turks have a Harem ; the Vifir himfelf has no
Seraglio.—The Ambaffadors of crowned heads have
each a Seraglio, but no Harem ; the Grand Signior
has both one and the other.

reftrains

restrains the Turks to four wives *nikiahlus*, or married ; but a Mahometan marriage is only a civil act, a contract executed before the Judge, who, in this case, officiates only as a common notary. The dowry, as well as the marriage-gift, the most important object, are specified in this act, which are returned to her in case of repudiation, and this act they call *nikaih*.'

There is another sort of marriage too, which allots a specific sum to be restored, and fixes a given period for the separation. This contract they call *kapin*; and is, properly speaking, no other than a bargain between the parties, to live together for a certain time, for a certain sum *.

By another law called *namekrem*, marriageable girls are forbid to uncover their

---

* Whenever one man has the privilege of taking and locking up forty women, the nine and thirty men who by this unfair division are deprived of the sweetest consolations humanity is blessed with, necessarily require some attention. We find, in consequence, that wherever a law has been made contrary to nature, another law becomes necessary to counteract it. From this we may deduce the origin of the marriages called *kapin*, of places of refuge for debtors, and foundling hospitals. Governments are like those frenetic gamesters who are constantly beating themselves, without correcting their errors.

faces,

faces, and married women, to any other than their hufbands. This law is not very favourable, undoubtedly, to marriages of inclination. A Turk marries his neighbour's daughter, or widow, without knowing her. He has no other method of determining his choice, than from the report of his other wives, or of fome mediatrix.

A moment's reflection is enough to fhow us, that the law of *namekrem* can never be fo rigidly obferved by the women of the lower clafs, who are conftantly following their occupations, as by the opulent and inactive. The working man, therefore, has fometimes the advantage of his own eyes to direct his choice, as a compenfation for the want of fortune, which puts it out of his power to avail himfelf of the right of plurality. Misfortune is generally balanced by fome advantage. But the abufe of good fortune has not the fame fource of confolation.

Such is the cafe with the plurality of wives, which neceffarily occafions unavoidable expences ; and where is the man in a fituation to fupport them ?

Except-

Excepting thofe who are in trade, and who, rich from their œconomy, ought not to be claffed among the luxurious, the Turks arrive at opulence, only from public employments, obtained through the favour of the great, who have raifed themfelves by the fame means. Their fortune is merely perfonal, accumulated by rapacioufnefs, hidden under ground on the flighteft alarm, diffipated in luxury, and fortuitoufly renewed; and their anxiety to acquire, and lavifh it, is fharpened by the perpetual precarioufnefs of their fituation.

The Turks feldom leave large fortunes to their children. Sums of money fo confiderable as to admit of being divided, would be temptations fufficient for the grafping hands of the fovereign, who would readily find a pretext in the manner by which they were acquired, to juftify his violence, in making himfelf mafter of their wealth.

A Turk, therefore, cannot in general be rich enough to maintain a confiderable harem, until he has obtained, through the favour of his patron, fome place of great
truft;

truft ; and which becomes lucrative in proportion to his abufe of authority.

Until that happens, confounded with the croud of young men, attached to the fame mafter, from the fame motives of ambition, reduced to the neceffity of living only amongft men, hurried on by the violence of his paffions, feparated from the women, yet inflamed by their proximity even in yielding to her impulfe, he is obliged to deviate from nature.

We have already feen, that fuch Turkifh women as are not to be procured on any other terms than marriage, and are not previoufly to be feen, are under the fame neceffity of living amongft themfelves. In fuch a cafe, what muft be their education? Born in opulence, they are either the daughters of a lawful wife, or of fome flave, the favourite of a moment. Their brothers and fifters are of different mothers, who differ in no refpect from flaves collected in the fame houfe. Occupied only by that jealoufy which animates them, one againft another, fcarcely knowing how to read or write, and reading nothing but the Coran ; expofed in the hot baths to all the inconveniencies of a forced perfpiration, too frequently repeated not to deftroy the frefhnefs of their fkin, and the grace of their contours, even before the age of puberty; indolent from pride, and often humbled by the inefficacy of the means pradtifed under their eyes to gratify their proprietor; deftined, in fhort, themfelves to the fame fate, without a hope of more fuccefs, in what can fuch women contri- bute to render the man happy who may chance to marry them? But it is not from that fource that he looks for happinefs. Let us fee then, whether he has made a better eftimate of the advantage of multiplying thofe flaves who have a right to choofe; whom he may marry without ceremony; and over whom he poffeffes, no doubt, a more precious right—the right of reftoring them to their freedom.

It is here that I wifh to draw the atten- tion to thofe Georgian and Circaffian flaves, whofe beauty has been fo often ce- lebrated; and it is perhaps of more impor- tance to afcertain the laws of flavery in Turkey, where the manners are already culpable enough, without fuffering a vague and erroneous opinion to add ftill further to their atrocity.

Neither

Neither the Greeks, the Armenians, nor even the Jews, are more liable than the Turks, to a conftitutional flavery. The defpotifm of the Sultan himfelf, however ftrong his paffion for her, does not enable him to take violent poffeffion of a young woman ; and though the Grecian blood ftill continues to produce as beautiful female forms as ferved for models to Praxiteles, the Turkifh annals do not furnifh an example of fuch atrocious violence.

Georgia and Circaffia are no more fubject to flavery, than any other province more directly under the dominion of the Grand Signior * ; but the want of lawful right is fupplied by the right of conqueft, which procured for the Turks near twenty thoufand flaves, who were carried off by the Kam of the Tartars from New Servia ; the greateft part of whom were reftored to Ruffia at the peace. *Krim Gueray*, who commanded that expedition, had, from the fame principle of right, laid wafte

* Georgia is rather one of the dependencies of Perfia than of Turkey ; but Prince Heraclius has availed himfelf of the troubles which have laid wafte the dominions of his fovereign, to enjoy a fort of independence.

Moldavia

Moldavia on a former occafion, without refpecting the Grand Signior's territory. The fame right of war obtains in Turkey, when a whole revolted province is given up to pillage, and its inhabitants reduced to flavery. This is the *droit public*, or *jus publicum* throughout all Afia ; and it is on thefe barbarous principles that one half of the globe is ftill governed, and that Georgia and Circaffia continue to furnifh with flaves, the market of Conftantinople *.

The incurfions of the Lefguis Tartars provide it with a regular fupply : Thefe Tartars inhabit the country between the Cafpian and the Black Sea, between Georgia and Circaffia ; and are in a perpetual ftate of warfare with thefe two provinces. They convey their flaves to the eaftern coaft of the Black Sea, and fell them to the Turkifh merchants, who refort there at ftated periods. The inhabitants of that coaft carry off alfo their own coun-

* The idea attached to a handfome Georgian or Circaffian flave, may be reduced to this ;—all the flaves in Turkey who are tolerably beautiful, muft be either Georgians or Circaffians ; but this, by no means, proves that they are all handfome.

trymen

trymen from the neighbouring villages, and make a trade of felling them ; and it is afferted, that even the parents, not unfrequently, make a traffic of their own children.

A country colder from its mountainous fituation, than from its latitude ; inhabited by people, fo wretched as to fell their own offspring ; fo ill-regulated as to fuffer them to be ftolen ; fo weak as to become an eafy prey to foreign plunderers, is not likely to poffefs in itfelf any fort of refinement or education. The children, therefore, are the only flaves whofe beauty can be cultivated, and who are capable of acquiring the graces. The avarice of the merchant will pay particular attention to this object ; and he will even endeavour to increafe the value of his flave, by fome agreeable accomplifhment, and an indecent dance, accompanied by caftinets, will be the ftrongeft recommendation.

Lady Mary Montague fays, that thefe dances are voluptuous. For my own part, I have feen them in their higheft perfection, performed by proficients in the art ; yet, although I am at a lofs for a proper term

term to characterife them, I fhould never think of calling them voluptuous.

And, I may further add, that the women dancers are defpifed in Turkey ; and that a flave, as foon as fhe has pleafed her mafter by this talent, ceafes to exercife it.

So that, in fact, they only ferve to awaken and excite the paffions of thofe machines, on whom indecency produces more effect than beauty. The graces, vivacity, and expreffion, poffefs alone the art of feducing us, exclufive even of regularity of features; whilft a liftlefs dignity, a profound ignorance, give a certain infipidity even to finifhed beauty. And this is the effect which the Turkifh women produce on their mafters.

I have had the opportunity of perfonal information from my Turkifh friends, that except in the inftance of fome new flave, who may excite their curiofity, the harem infpires them only with difguft. A great many Turks never enter their harem, but to reftore tranquillity, when the female fuper-intendant is unequal to the tafk ; but let the punifhment be ever fo fevere, it is impoffible to eradicate the caufes of this irregularity. Thefe diforders, arifing from
the

the confinement and affemblage of many wives, are another confequence of the law of plurality. Nature counteracted equally in either fex, muft neceffarily lead both aftray.

This exclufive fociety of the women produces alfo this effect, that being conftantly obferved by their companions, they do not even endeavour to diffemble, either their tafte or their jealoufy ; they have only to conceal ther quarrels. Too fortunate, indeed, if nature calmed, gratified, and deceived, does not urge them to efcape from their prifon, to run, after the reality ; an excefs of which they are invariably the victims, and which I fhall hereafter have occafion to mention.

But, however the cuftoms of the country may have reftricted the Turkifh women, it muft not be imagined that they are without the power of fending their flaves, or of going out themfelves, to purchafe what they want ; I do not know a fingle Turk who deprives them of that liberty ; nay, they very frequently go out together to walk, or pay a vifit in other harems ; and in the latter cafe, the etiquette obliges the Turk, for whofe wives the

the visit is intended, not to enter his harem during the stay of the visitants. But how many methods are there of evading this regulation ; and if the parties be well inclined, who is there to insist on its being regularly observed ?

But because the streets are filled with women, who pass freely to and fro on business, and the harems the most closely shut, are not unfrequently thrown open, to let the flock, confined in them, amuse themselves with a walk ; we must not thence conclude, with Lady Mary Montague, that the intrigues are carried on in the shops, into which the women sometimes enter : they would there be too easily observed. It is in the country, in retired situations, on the borders of the sea, that their gallantries actually take place; heedless of the danger of being discovered by the guards, who are always prying into the most concealed retirements.

The *Bostandgy Bachi*, whose authority always extends several leagues around the Grand Signior's residence, has, in fact, the inspection of these so much talked of affairs of gallantry, and exercises, in that respect, the office of Lieutenant of Police.

It

It is the moſt important perquiſite of his employment, and is attended with the moſt frightful abuſes. But I ſhall have occaſion to ſpeak further of this in the courſe of my obſervations, and I have already ſaid enough of the Turkiſh women, to prepare my reader for what remains upon that ſubject.

C 5

MEMOIRS

MEMOIRS

OF THE

BARON de TOTT.

FIRST PART.

THE death of Sultan Mahomout,. and of M. D'Salleurs,. determined the Court of France to fend M. de Ver-gennes to Conftantinople ; and I was or-dered to accompany him, to learn the lan-guage, and to ftudy the manners and go-vernment of the Turks. We embarked at Marfeilles, in a veffel freighted by the King, from whence we fet fail at the be-ginning of April, 1755 ; but contrary winds prevented us from reaching the Dar-danelles until the 18th of May. Before we arrived at the Streight, we perceived a cara-

caravelle * belonging to the Grand Signior, at anchor oppofite to Tenedos, and her felucca, which was fent to reconnoitre, bearing down, and fhe came up with us oppofite the coaft of Troy; but fearing the plague, we were defirous of avoiding all communication with them. My late father, whom the King fent with M. de Vergennes to Conftantinople, where he had already been feveral times, and who fpoke the language, prevailed on the Turks not to come on board, and thought it proper to reward the officer who commanded the felucca, with a few bottles of cordial: The cabin-boy who went to feek for this prefent, brought up fix bottles of lavender water, and was ordered to rectify the miftake; but my father declaring that it was perfectly the fame thing, we gave them the lavender water, and parted company; but the impatience of the Turk foon attracted our attention: he feized on one of the phials, broke off the neck, emptied it at one draught, and turning round made us a fign of approbation. We were all afraid, except my father, that the poor fellow

* A Turkifh veffel of war.

fellow would fall backwards; but were very foon made eafy on his account, on feeing him open, and empty, a fecond phial with the fame tokens of fatisfaction.

Very foon after we entered the Streight of the Dardanelles, and furled our colours, to avoid the falute from the caftles, and the Captain Pacha *, whofe fleet was at anchor off Gallipoli ; and we caft anchor at length in the port of Conftantinople, the 21ft of May, 1755.

This city, fituated at the eaftern extremity of Europe, near the Black Sea, is only feparated from Afia by the Thracian Bofphorus. The canal which forms a communication between two feas, pours into the fouthern part, the fuperfluous wa‑ters which rufh from the North into the Black Sea, and which its furface is unable to evaporate. To this effect, the currents are violent down the canal, and bear on the point of the Seraglio which forms a Cape, that divides, and intercepts one part of the waters, which, after having circu-lated in the harbour, return by the oppo-

* The Turkifh Admiral.

fite

fite fhore, and re-enter their former bed.
It is owing to this mechanifm of Nature,
that the harbour of Conftantinople is cleared of all its rubbifh, and of the filth that is
daily thrown into it.   The fea in this cafe
operating for herfelf, what ignorance never
could forefee, and fhips of eighty guns can
lay a plank on the fhore without any danger.

If the ambition of governing the univerfe fearched for a fituation the moft favourable for eftablifhing a capital of the
world, that of Conftantinople, as repre-
fented on the map, would undoubtedly
have the preference. Situated between two
feas, this city would form at once the centre of the moft ufeful productions, and
of the moft flourifhing commerce, were
it not for the preffure of that defpotifm
which, for twenty leagues around, breaks
in pieces every inftrument of culture, and
of induftry.   Shut up within the limits of
its ancient walls, Conftantinople, on the
land fide, offers to the traveller nothing
but the appearance of deftruction; whilft
the navigator, placed in the centre of an
immenfe amphi-theatre, feems to croud

from

from all parts to bring the tribute which the univerfe owes to its metropolis.

The ancient Byzantium, whofe walls at prefent form the enclofure of the Grand Signior's Seraglio, fituated on the extremity of the Cape which fhuts in the harbour, prefents a foreft of cyprefs trees, overtopped by an infinite number of leaden cupolas, enriched with golden balls, the whole forming a pyramid, with the tower of the Divan, which crowns the fummit: This dufky groupe appears detached from the reft of the landfcape, which is only varied by fome large fcattered buildings of too heavy an architecture for the furrounding objects.

The harbour, from the point of the Seraglio, to the frefh water *, renders one

* The fmall river which falls into the fea at the bottom of the harbour, and waters the Valley of Kiathana, is fo called. The Grand Signior has a Kiofk in that valley; and Sultan Achmet, pretending to imitate Marly, invited all his Court to build on the two declivities which form the banks of the river; but thefe buildings were deftroyed by the rebels who depofed Sultan Achmet. The prejudices of the Turks, invariably at enmity with all European imitations, were the pretext for this deftruction; the real motive was the love of plunder.

fide

side of the triangle, formed by Conftantinople, two thoufand toifes longer than the
others : on the oppofite fhore are immenfe
fuburbs, which, including the town of
Galata, furnifh a landfcape, whofe richnefs is ftill further increafed and varied by
the continued chain of villages that join
and are confounded together on the banks
of the Bofphorus, even to within fix leagues
of the Black Sea. Thefe buildings are continued on the fide of Afia, and unite at
Scutary; which place, fituated three quarters of a league from the entrance of the
harbour, offers to Conftnatinople itfelf, a
moft interefting profpect. The boats that
are continually traverfing the fpace between the two towns, feem to form a junc-
tion, Europe with Afia. Other veffels are
employed every morning to tranfport the
inhabitants of the villages of the Bofphorus
to their labours in the capital, by which
they are maintained, and to convey them
home every evening; befides which, an infinite number of fmaller boats are paffing
in every direction to fupply the occafional
wants of the inhabitants; and if to this
be added, the tranfport veffels daily arriving with provifions for the capital, from
the

the Black Sea and the Archipelago, and the general activity of the foreign commerce that fupplies this city with luxuries and cloathing from every quarter of the world, one can fcarcely conceive the beauty of this perpetually moving picture.

But if nothing can equal the profpect of Conftantinople from without, the charm foon vanifhes on entering the town: the greateft part of the ftreets fo narrow, as that the projection of the roofs fcarcely leaves admiffion for the light ; a pavement of pebbles badly taken care of; and no attention to cleanlinefs: thefe are amongft the difagreeable circumftances of that capital. But I fhall referve the particulars of other inconveniencies, as they occur occafionally, and in fucceffion.

Convinced that the ftudy of the Turkifh language could alone give me an infight into the manners and cuftoms of that people, I made it my firft object; and I would not liften to thofe who advifed me to begin by reading the travellers who have treated on the oriental nations ; for it ftruck me, that I had more to apprehend from the danger of adopting their errors, than would

com-

compenſate for any time and trouble they might ſave me.

My Turkiſh maſter began by teaching me to write, which is their method. The knowledge I had of drawing, helped me in my progreſs; at length I was able to read, and then my difficulties began to multiply: the ſuppreſſion of the vowels * is ſufficient to give an idea of my firſt embarraſſment, and of the difficult and irkſome taſk I had undertaken; but this is not all; the Turks, to ſupply the poverty of their language, have entirely adopted the Arabic and Perſian; and by compoſing five alphabets, the different characters of which are at the arbitrary diſpoſal of the writer, have thrown freſh obſtacles in the way of inſtruction; ſo that if the life of a man be ſcarcely ſufficient to learn to read well, what time will there remain for him to ſelect his authors, or to profit by what he has read?

---

* The vowels being only expreſſed by ſigns placed without the body of the writing, the writers leave them to be ſupplied by the ingenuity of the reader; from thence ariſe many literary diſputes on the conſonants, the uſe of which may change the ſenſe: but to avoid the danger of ſuch diſcuſſions of the Coran, that book is never written without vowels.

The

The ignorance of the Turks in every thing that concerns the abftract fciences, muft be attributed, in great meafure, to this inconvenience : wholly occupied in painting well, and in decyphering their characters, their conceitednefs gives them a turn for difficulties of that kind; a double meaning, the tranfpofition of letters forms the extent of their ftudies, and their literature; and every thing that can be inverted by falfe tafte, to fatigue the mind, conftitutes their delight, and excites their admiration.

My language mafter, of Perfian extraction, and a great enthufiaft in poetry, ufed to get drunk indifferently with opium, or with brandy; and I paffed two hours every day in this agreeable téte à téte. I employed myfelf particularly in making ufe of all the words I could ftore up in my memory; and I was no fooner able to underftand him, than he afked me one day, with great earneftnefs, what fmell it was he had perceived on entering my apartment? I fhewed him a bottle of lavender water; and the example of the captain of the felucca induced me to confent to make the facrifice which he defired, without hefitation;

and

and which he bore without fuffering the flighteft inconvenience. I did not think proper, however, to continue to fupply him with fo dangerous a draught.

My application to collect a number of words; and above all, my anxiety to employ them, enabled me, in a very fhort time, to explain myfelf very tolerably; and I was already able to do without an interpreter, when M. de Vergennes gave orders to prepare an entertainment intended for the foreign minifters, and all the Europeans fettled at Conftantinople. This excited the curiofity of fome Turks of diftinction, who were defirous of being prefent; and I undertook to do the honours to them, the more readily from the frefh opportunity it afforded me of practifing their language.

I was newly married, and the intimacy that fubfifted between the principal perfon amongft thofe Turks, and my father-in-law, added greatly to that favourable opinion with which my zeal for information had already infpired him. On his arrival, he begged me to point out to him Madam de Tott from amongft the ladies; and becoming very foon attentive to her moft

trifling

trifling motions, he followed her with his eyes, and appeared uneafy, if in the croud, fhe efcaped an inftant from his fight. Excepting this anxiety, the coup d'œil of the entertainment appeared to.ally to abforb my Turks, who put various queftions to me on this new fcene, not lefs amufing than inftructive.

The ball is opened by a minuet ; I am afked who is the gentleman that dances ?—It is the Swedifh Envoy. " What !" fays the Turk to me with furprize, " the Envoy from Sweden ?—The Minifter of a Court in alliance with the Sublime Porte ! —No, that is impoffible.—You are miftaken ;—look again." " I am not miftaken," faid I, " it is he ; yes, it is he himfelf." The Turk at length convinced, caft down his eyes, fell into reflection, and was filent until the end of that minuet, which was followed by another. A frefh queftion to know the dancer ? " It is the Dutch Ambaffador." " Oh ! as for that," fays the Turk, gravely, " I never will believe it. I know very well," continued he, " to what a heighth the Ambaffador of France can carry his magnificence ; and notwithftanding my furprize,

I can

I can carry that idea fo far as to conceive that he is rich enough to make a minifter of the fecond order dance; but at what price can he obtain that fervice from an Ambaffador? There cannot, poffibly, exift between them fo enormous a difference." I made ufe of all the Turkifh words I knew to explain to him, that thefe minifters were the object of the entertainment; that they were not paid for that purpofe, but danced for their pleafure; and that the Ambaffador of France himfelf would dance: with difficulty I convinced him. Another object, however, which he undoubtedly thought more interefting, very foon occupied his attention. "I do not fee your wife!" faid he, "Oh! yes; there fhe is; but fomebody is talking to her! Run and interrupt the converfation." "Why fo?" faid I. He then explained himfelf more clearly; and I was endeavouring to fatisfy him, when Madam de Tott, continuing her converfation, went into the room where the company was at play, and difappeared. Seeing this, the Turk lofing all patience, rifes, and draws me after him. I fuffered him to draw me along, and foon found that the fight of

feveral

several tables, where the men were disputing about play, was not the spectacle with which his friendship had alarmed him on my account.

Supper was served, and my friend seeing the company place themselves at different tables, was inclined to go. An uneasiness of a more serious nature appeared to agitate him. I pressed him to stay till the end of the entertainment. " Every thing finished," said he briskly ; " they are preparing to drink. Permit us to go; and if you will follow my advice, take your wife, and withdraw likewise." " I understand you," said I ; " but do not be uneasy ; every thing will pass more peaceably than you imagine." I insisted upon it, and succeeded in conducting my curious friends around all the tables, and in making them sit down at that which was prepared for them. A few glasses of cordial gave them courage, and completely gained them ; they staid till morning, and gave me to understand, that if such an entertainment were to be given amongst them, it would not terminate without thirty murders.

The

The knowledge I began to acquire of their character, induced me to form fuch connections as were capable of extending it. Amongst thofe whofe acquaintance I more particularly cultivated, was Murad Mollach, of the family of Damat Zade, which from the period of the conqueft of Conftantinople, has, in every generation, given Muftis to the empire ; and who was himfelf deftined for that dignity. I fhall very often have occafion to fpeak of this perfon ; and the obfervations I fhall make on him, will ferve to elucidate the charac-ter of his nation.

To follow, as nearly as poffible, the chain of events to which I have been a witnefs, let us caft an eye on thofe confla-grations which ravage Conftantinople too frequently not to deferve to be mentioned. I fhall felect the moft ftriking inftance of this kind ; I mean the fire which confumed two thirds of that immenfe city a fhort time after our arrival.

The Palace of France, fituated in the fuburb of Pera, overlooks the town and harbour of Conftantinople. The fire broke out in the morning near to the fhore and the walls of the Seraglio. The wind,
which

which was northerly, made the fire run along thefe walls; and about feven o'clock reached the Palace of the Vifir, ſituated on the middle of the hill. The Grand Signior was prefent; but neither his orders, nor the efforts which were made to prevent it, could fave that vaft building from the flames; and the focus which it formed gave new activity to them. The fire continued to extend itfelf in the direction of the wind, with the greateft rapidity. We were in hopes, however, that in approaching the church of St. Sophia, the mafs of that building would ftop the conflagration; and accordingly all the fuccours were directed to that quarter, in expectation of ftopping the progrefs of the flames; but the lead of the cupola, melted by the heat of the atmofphere, running through the ftone gutters on the heads of the guards and workmen, left a full fcope to the activity of the fire. From that moment, nobody thought of ftopping it; and it was fuffered to devour every thing which fell in its way in the direction of the wind, as far as the walls of the Admiralty, on the other fide of the hill. The confternation was general; yet every one congratulated himfelf

VOL. I.   D   at

at feeing the fire arrived at that period ;
when the wind fhifting round with violence to the eaft, carried that line of fire
acrofs the town for more than twelve hundred toifes, (or about feven thoufand eight
hundred Englifh feet;) the flames then
rufhing towards the center of the city,
formed thirteen diftinct branches of fire,
the roots of which fucceffively uniting,
Conftantinople very foon became a burning fea.

The efforts which were then made, inftead of being ferviceable, only added to
the calamity : a whole regiment of Janiffaries, employed in beating down fome
houfes, at the head of one of the branches,
were furrounded by two lateral branches,
of the fire. The cries of the unfortunate
wretches conveyed through the column of
fire, with thofe of the women and children who were fuffering the fame fate ; the
crafh of the falling buildings ; the crack-
ling of the flaming planks, which were
carried into the air by the violence of the
heat ; the tumult of the inhabitants, threatened by the conflagration in every quarter,
and who, to fecure themfelves from the
moft dreadful mifery, were expofing their
lives

lives to fave a part of their effects; every thing confpired to render it a fcene, the accumulated horror of which is not to be defcribed.

But it is ftill more inconceivable, that the rebuilding of thefe houfes was not yet completed, before a frefh fire confumed them, without the inhabitants having it in their power to ufe any precaution for their fafety. Sultan Ofman, then upon the Throne, ftrove in vain to enlarge fome of the ftreets, and open fome new ones, to facilitate the neceffary affiftance: The proprietors joined in infifting on the entire poffeffion of the ground left them by their fathers. The government which had only known how to give orders when it was neceffary to pay, was fo weak as to give way to this oppofition, which might have been fo eafily furmounted. Such is defpotifm.

It might have been forefeen, that the robberies which are eafily committed under the pretence of giving affiftance to the houfes in the neighbourhood of the fire, had very often been the caufe of thofe conflagrations; and the government thinking to remedy that evil, by forbidding any perfon to endeavour to extinguifh them until

the

the arrival of the principal officers, only contribute to increafe it. It was, in fact, giving time to the flames to acquire activity. That law, therefore, was abolifhed, the number of fire-engines augmented, and inftead of being kept, as heretofore, at the houfes of the governors of each quarter, were diftributed to the different guard-houfes, from whence the guards had orders to convey them on the firft alarm. But what were the confequences of this regulation? That the perfons who have the management of the engines, difplayed their activity with no other view than to extort money for the protection of the unfortunate, and to play upon the croud for their amufement; that the guards, familiarized with thefe difafters, make a fport of them, and add to the public mifery, by ill treating the wretched fufferers; that the workmen inconfiderately throw into the fire, inftead of removing the materials, which feed the flame, and that the multitude are intent upon plundering on all fides *.

The

* The law has condemned the robbers in this fort of pillage to be thrown into the flames; but the habit

The Vifir, and all the great officers of the Porte, are obliged to appear on the fpot, on the firft intelligence of fire, to give the neceffary directions. The Grand Signior himfelf never fails to appear if the fire makes any progrefs: the means of conveying him are ready on the firft fignal; he has a number of horfes faddled, night and day, and armed boats ready for that purpofe. The great officers ufe the fame precaution, and thefe difagreeable expeditions, which are frequent, very often interrupt their fleep.

It is the duty of the guardians of the quarters, who are called *Paffevans*, to watch for fires during the night. They run through their diftrict, armed with large flicks, tipped with iron, which they ftrike

bit of beholding a number of wretches perifh in that way, from the frequency and rapidity of the fires, produces this effect, that the danger to which one is every day expofed onefelf, confidered as a punifhment, is from that circumftance, reduced pretty nearly to the misfortune of dying in one's bed. The fevereft punifhments alone will never eftablifh good order: it is the refult of an enlightened attention, which defpotifm never makes ufe of.

againft

againft the pavement, and awaken the
people with the cry of *yangen vor*; or, there
is a fire; and point out the quarter where
it has appeared.   A very high tower in the
palace of the Janiffary Aga, as well as another at Galata, overlook all Conftantinople; and there is a guard in each of thefe
towers, conftantly looking out for the fame
object.   It is there that a fort of 'larum,
formed by beating two large drums, quick-
ens the alarm, and conveys it rapidly down
the canal, from whence a vaft concourfe
of perfons who are interefted run to their
fhops, as they often find them burnt or
pillaged.

It is for this reafon that the Befeftins
have been built, either by the body of merchants, or by individuals, who let out the
warehoufes, as places of fecurity for the
more precious merchandife, out of the
reach of the flames, or to preferve them
from plunder, in cafe of an infurrection,
or a fire.   Thefe buildings, which ferve at
the fame time as ftreets, are built of hewn
ftone, and vaulted the whole length with
brick.   Each of them contains articles nearly of the fame kind; but if thofe of the
goldfmith are of the moft value, it is neither

from

from their tafte, nor workmanfhip. I fhall
have occafion in another place to fpeak of
the induftry of the Turks.

After the misfortune of which I have
been fpeaking, the refidence of the Grand
Signior's Minifters was transferred, until
the palace of the Grand Vifir fhould be
rebuilt, to the palace of a Sultana, which
had efcaped the fire ; and M. de Vergennes, who had hitherto borne only the title
of Envoy of France, having obtained that
of Ambaffador, prepared to deliver his new
credentials.

Said Effendi, the fame who had been
Ambaffador in France, was at that time
Grand Vifir. We went to his audience,
without intending to go to that of the
Grand Signior before the fecond Tuefday,
the firft being too near * ; but the Sultan,
who

* The Grand Signior never gives audience to Ambaffadors but on Tuefdays, which is the day of the
Divan of the Seraglio. He ftays on the ground-floor
of a fquare tower, which bears his name. The Vifir,
as well as the great Judges of Europe and of Afia, the
Grand Treafurer, &c. are feated on benches, which
go round the hall. Above the Vifir's feat, oppofite
to the gate, is a fmall window, with bars, and raifed
about nine or ten feet, from whence the Grand Signior

who was incognito at the Porte *, gave M. de Vergennes to underſtand that he wonld receive him the next day. This Prince, of a paſſionate, but feeble charac- ter, impatient, and curious to exceſs, af- forded us on our return a very ſingular ex- hibition. We found him diſguiſed as a man of the law, and accompanied only by his Seliċtar †, and his Devitdar ‡, both diſguiſed as Tchoadars §. He had ſtopt in one of the ſtreets, to ſee us paſs, and the line of our march lying through the *At- meydan* ‖, we very ſoon ſaw the Prince, ſometimes running by the ſide of us, and at others ſhortening his pace near the Ambaſ- ſador, whom he accompanied to the end of

nior can hear every thing which paſſes in the Divan, but from whence, as he is made to believe, he nei- ther can be poniarded, nor can he poniard any other perſon.

* This ſignifies the reſidence of the Viſir, where all the public offices are kept, and all the other officers of the Porte ſit in the day time, to carry on the affairs of their reſpeċtive departments.

† The Sword-bearer, who executes the office of Grand Chamberlain, and Captain of the Guards.

‡ Secretary, and Keeper of the Royal papers.

§ Servants who attend their maſters on foot.

‖ Place of the Hippodromos.

that

that place, when again running on, he paffed the ftreet at the head of the firft line of
people, and entering by one of the gates
of the garden of the Seraglio, went out
towards the Admiralty, to fall in with us
again on the Pier *, where we embarked,
and where he remained till our departure,
after which he re-entered, and we loft fight
of him.

I could not help remarking, that during
the whole time this Prince accompanied us
in the place of the Hippodromos, where
our appearance had attracted many curious
people, not one of them made the fmalleft
movement tending to him, though there
was not one of them who did not know
him, and who was not terrified at his prefence.   But it is the nature of defpotifm to
command, and to make them diffemble
even their very fears.

I fhall not enter into a detail of the ce-
remonial of the Grand Signior's audience:
travellers have already faid enough of it to
make me filent, on the fubject of the various humiliations that Ambaffadors expe-

* A fort of jettee of ftone, or planks on piles, to
facilitate the approach of boats for the purpofe of embarkation and difembarkation.

rience

rience on fuch occafions : it will be more useful to difcufs the methods of avoiding them ; and I defcribe only the manners of the Turks.

It was remarkable, however, in this audience, that the Grand Signior, inftead of addreffing himfelf to his Vifir, to convey his anfwer, addreffed himfelf directly to M. de Vergennes, to whom the Drogman of the Porte tranflated it, and which was conceived in terms full of efteem for that Ambaffador, and by no means framed on principles of etiquette. This anfwer could not have been premeditated, but proceeded fpontaneoufly, from a fort of affability in the Prince.

Sultan Ofman, in other refpects little capable of that energy fo often neceffary to a defpotic fovereign, made up for this deficiency by an habitual impatience and frequent fits of paffion. Selictar-Pacha, young, full of confidence, and proud of the favour of his mafter, who had raifed him to the Vifiriate, thought he might give himfelf up, without fear and without reftraint, to fuch violent meafures, as, from their frequent repetition, excited a general murmur. Thefe

com-

complaints, which always with difficulty reach the Throne, came very readily to the knowledge of the Sultan, in the walks he took incognito ; and that Prince, enraged at his favourite, made him attend at the Seraglio, in prefence of the Mufti, whom he had fent for on the occafion. The violence of his paffion was fo great, that laying hold of a pile of arms, he would himfelf have ftruck him, had not the chief of the law interpofed. To reftrain his firft emotion, increafed no doubt the anger of Sultan Ofman ; for his victim was very foon difpatched, and the Vifir ordered out of the inner apartment ; but followed by an order, was ftopped between the two gates *. The Soliétar-Aga took from him the feal of the empire, and his head, ftruck off upon the fpot, was expofed on a filver plate at the gate of the fecond Court, be-

* The paffage from the firft court of the Seraglio into the fecond is fhut in by two gates, between which there are apartments in the towers, which flank the entry ; the Porters occupy a part of it, but the principal apartment is called the Dgellate Odaffi, the Hangman's Chamber.

fore

fore there was the leaft fufpicion of this firft minifter's lofs of favour †.

The Ulemats, that celebrated body of lawyers, who never fail to feize the feeble remains of authority, to opprefs authority itfelf, who had until then been kept under fubjection by the influence of the Vifir, imagined, that after his death, they could bear their fway with more impunity. The Ulemats, in fact, abufed the weaknefs of the Sultan to fuch a degree, as could not fail of drawing down his vengeance on that body, and his fury broke forth againft the Mufti.

Fanaticifm, which every where produces fanguinary, or abfurd laws, and often both, has eftablifhed one in Turkey in favour of thefe Ulemats, by which their property cannot be confifcated, nor can they be punifhed with death in any other way than by pounding them in a mortar. One does not very well fee the pleafure of fuch a pre-eminence; but it is not difficult to perceive that the examples of fo terrible a punifhment muft be lefs frequent, from

† There was a writing likewife in the following words:—" It is thus all perfons are treated who abufe the favour of their mafter."

the

the intereft thefe men of the law have in preventing their repetition. It was, without doubt, under the idea of this impunity, that the Mufti received with infolence the menaces of his mafter; and this refiftance irritated Sultan Ofman fo much, that he ordered the mortars to be dug up which had been buried by length of time. This order alone produced the moft decided effect. The body of Ulemats, juftly terrified, were all fubmiffion, and the famous Rachub Pacha, who was appointed Vifir, governed without oppofition.

Rachub united to the moft engaging manners, great ftrength of character. Never did a Vifir poffefs more the talents neceffary for his fituation. He knew how to corrupt with addrefs, and to overawe the moft audacious; always treacherous, always malignant, but always able, and perfect mafter of himfelf, he fet little value upon mankind, and looked upon their lives as nothing.

This Minifter had formerly been Pacha of Cairo, the place in all the empire the leaft adapted to his character. The undifciplined ftate of the Bey-Mamelucs, propped up however by force, had left him no other

other refource but corruption for his fupport, without being the lefs expofed to
acts of violence. He had juft efcaped from
the fhot of a piftol, fired at him in his
own Divan, when the Grand Signior called him to the Vifirate. Rachub joined to
all the talents neceffary to defpotifm, the
moft ufeful general knowledge of the affairs of the empire, which he had acquired
at the treaty of Belgrade, when he had
filled the poft of Mektoubtchy *.

The various employments through which
this Minifter had fucceffively paffed, leaving no perfon the hope of becoming neceffary to him, he found every body difpofed to be fubfervient to his will; and it
was very foon remarked, that the habit of
authority had taught him to exprefs his orders in a very wanton manner.

The interval between the death of Selictar Pacha, and the elevation of Rachub
to the Vifirate, had been filled by a great
number of Vifirs, fome of whom were not
fifteen days in office. We were tired of

---

* Mektoubtchy is a Minifter of the Porte of the
fecond order: This place can only be compared to
that of the firft Clerk of the firft Minifter, if fuch a
one exifted.

the

the frequent audiences occafioned by thefe changes, but it was neceffary, neverthe-lefs, to appear at that of the new Minifter. The ceremonies ufual on thefe occafions were at an end; but Rachub was continu-ing a friendly converfation with the Am-baffador, when the Muzar Aga * coming into the hall, and approaching the Pacha, whifpered a word in his ear. We obferv-ed very plainly that the only anfwer he re-ceived was by a flight horizontal movement of the hand; after which his Highnefs im-mediately refuming an agreeable fmile, proceeded to converfe a few minutes longer with the Ambaffador. We left the hall of audience at length, to regain the bottom of the ftair-cafe, where we mounted our horfes, and nine heads cut off, and ranged on the outfide of the firft gate, explained to us in paffing, the meaning of the gef-ture which the Vifir made ufe of in our prefence.

The inutility of precipitating in fuch a manner an execution which he could com-mand at any time with the greateft eafe, may lead one to prefume, that this was

* This anfwers to the office of Grand Prevot in France.

pre-

preconcerted, in order to give us an opinion of the fpeedy juftice of the new Minifter, but we could difcover nothing in this fcene but its atrocity. This is the main-fpring of defpotifm ; it always overwhelms, but never punifhes: and thefe were the means conftantly employed by Rachub *.

But if the great men of the empire were compelled to fubmit to the ufe this Vifir made of his political principles, it was re-ferved for a woman of the lower clafs of the people to refift him with impunity ; and as the nature of the fedition fhe occafioned is connected with the fubfiftence of Conftan-tinople, it is important to lay open that part of the Turkifh adminiftration.

The Grand Signior, who makes a pub-lic monopoly of the corn, for the fupply of the capital, receives that article from the maritime provinces, where he has eftab-lifhed the impoft Tchetirach †, which con-

* Under a defpotic government, the exiftence of every man in place muft be neceffarily precarious ; and no one can there gratify his ambition by filling them, without being indifferent about his own life. What value can he then be fuppofed to fet on the lives of others ?

† The produce of this monopoly belongs to the Pub-lic Treafure : the management of it is entrufted to the Tefterdar (Grand Treafurer.)

fifts

fifts in an obligation to deliver to the Grand Signior, at a very low price, a ftipulated quantity of corn, which is conveyed into his ftore-houfes by veffels freighted for his account. This article he fells again in retail to the bakers who are obliged to receive and make ufe of it at the price fixed by his Highnefs. The neceffary confequence of this method of adminiftering affairs are, the prohibition of the exportation of corn, the unavoidable knavery of the officers, who evade the order, the perifhing of the grain which is ftored, and badly taken care of, very often unwholefome, and famine, is the laft refult.

Conftantinople was threatened with this calamity; bread diminifhed in weight was confiderably augmented in price; the bakers had even begun to adulterate it, and the only remaining hopes of a frefh fupply of corn, depended on the arrival of feventy veffels expected from the Black Sea; when intelligence was received of the lofs of all thofe veffels, caft away on the coaft, by miffing, in the night, the entrance of the Canal. Conftantinople was in confternation, and one cannot think, without horror, that this accident was occafioned by
a kind

a kind of abuse, which would not appear credible, did it not even now continue frequently to occur.

Two very lofty light-houses are placed at the mouth of the Black Sea, on the two promontories of Asia and of Europe, to point out the entrance of the Canal, to navigators. The government provides the oil necessary for the consumption, and guards are paid for 'the daily lighting and supplying them; but this government allows, at the same time, the making of charcoal along the whole coast, although they might have foreseen, that under this pretence the inhabitants would kindle fires capable of deceiving and misguiding the mariner, in stormy weather. They ought also to have known, that the guards of the two light-houses would intercept the light of the lantherns, that vessels might be cast away, and they profit by the wreck *.

The first method adopted by the government to remedy this misfortune, was by

---

* Humanity once abandoned to injustice, very soon makes a sport of every crime. One disorder always produces a greater, which is more certain when the laws authorize it by their example. Is there a legislator who ought not to tremble at this dilemma?

a genea general order throughout the empire to take the feed corn from the hufbandmen. The fubfequent diftreffes of which they were laying the foundation, were over-looked by the intereft of the moment; the fole intereft of defpotifm Not only the ground corn, but beans and all kinds of pulfe were feized on, and avarice, which avails itfelf of every event, got poffeffion of all forts of provifior, for the purpofe of adulterating its quality, yet without fup-plying the quantity demanded.

It became neceffary to place guards on the ovens, which were perpetually befieged by a famifhed people : a cake of dough, badly baked, was all that was delivered to each perfon ; and the Turks prefenting themfelves, piftol or fword in hand, com-mitted all forts of outrages.

In the midft of this diftrefs, which had occafioned the rice likewife to be hoarded, the firmnefs of the Vifir had hitherto main-tained a fort of tranquillity in the city, when a woman of the lower clafs, old, but fearlefs of danger, raifing a mob amongft the women of her quarter, very foon in-creafed her troop, and hurried towards the granaries of rice, infulting the guards, who
de-

demanded, on the road, the reason of this riotous affembly? The Janiffary Aga *, flies to the place with a numerous guard, but is repulfed by a fhower of ftones, the rice magazines are forced, and the pillage begun, when the Grand Signior arrives in perfon; the old woman advanced towards him, and infulted him with menaces, openly defying the power of his foldiers; fhe harangues him with intrepidity, prevails upon, or rather makes him feel the neceffity of giving way, obtains a portion of rice for each of her combatants, and difmiffes her victorious band.

The excefs of the abufes, however, which had produced a temporary reftoration of order, procured, for fome time, the fupply neceffary for commerce; the famine difappeared; but the difeafes arifing from the unwholefome nourifhment, adding to the exhalations of the plague, that dreadful fcourge began its ravages, and fpread throughout the empire.

The refearches which have been made into the caufes of that diforder, have been hitherto productive only of opinions, either

---

* The General of the Infantry.

con-

contradictory or belied by facts. It was thought to be of Egyptian origin ; but it will appear, from my obfervations made in thefe countries, that this laft conjecture is abfolutely without foundation.

But, whatever be the caufe or origin, the focus which preferves it, and the caufes by which it is propagated, are clearly afcertained. Both one and the other arife from the dealers in old cloaths, and the conduct of individuals, at Conftantinople, who preferve in their chefts, not only the cloaths, but even the furs of thofe who have died of the plague. This is taking, undoubtedly the moft effectual method to foment and perpetuate the feeds of the diforder. It attacks infallibly thofe perfons who are fufceptible of it from the ftate of their body, and its progrefs is more rapid in that feafon when the humours are in fermentation.

It was therefore towards the beginning of the fpring following the fcarcity, that the firft fymptoms of the plague began to make their appearance, which carried off, in that year, upwards of one hundred and fifty thoufand fouls in the city of Conftantinople alone; and the number of dead

was

was fo great, as to authorize public prayers to God for a ceffation of this calamity; for it may be proper to obferve, that the Turks bear it patiently, and without a murmur, until the daily lift of burials, which pafs through the fingle gate of Adrianople, amounts to 999. This is the ftated terms of their refignation!

'Neither the beginning, nor the different periods of this diftemper, excite any further attention than what arifes from the frequency of the burials; but this fcourge interrupts no bufinefs, and the movement occafioned by them keeps up the communication, and increafes the progrefs of the evil. There is no reafon, however, from obfervation, to imagine, that the air contributes toward it; and habit which familiarizes us with the greateft difafters, and the moft certain dangers, procures as ready an affiftance for the fick, as in the flighteft epidemical fevers. The Turks ftill find their greateft fecurity in a blind predeftination.

The Greeks, the Armenians, and the Jews, who do not carry this prejudice to the fame excefs, have ftudied a fort of remedy which they make ufe of with fome fuccefs,

fuccefs, but never until the firft attacks of the diftemper are allayed ; but it is remaikable that each of thefe nations has adopted a different regimen, peculiar to itfelf, and this fingularity muft be attributed, no doubt, to the difference in their food. It is, however, the fureft method not to adopt this fact, which is afferted by feveral phyficians, but for whofe credibility I will not anfwer.

The Europeans are the only perfons who take any precautions againft the infection ; long habit makes them too frequently neglectful, but never without the greateft rifque ; and thofe who are not compelled to an abfolute refidence, withdraw themfelves the more readily into the country during the plague ; as that diforder, which begins its ravages in the fpring, ufually laft until the beginning of winter. The Ifle of Princes, fituated five leagues from Conftantinople, at the entrance of the gulph which forms the Sea of Marmora, was the place to which the French formerly gave the preference ; they are fince difperfed in different villages on the borders of the Canal, on the European fide ; and the Ambaffadors in general, and the merchants

of

of every nation, reſide in the villages of Tarapia and Buyukdere; that of Belgrade, celebrated for the reſidence of Lady Mary Montague, was for a long time preferred; but the air, which is become unwhole-ſome, has made it loſe that preference.

I had made choice of the ſmall village of Keffely Keuy, to get out of the way of all communication during the plague, of which I have been ſpeaking. This village is ſituated near to Buyukdere, where Mu-rad Mollach had his ſummer reſidence, and took ſome liberties to the great ſcandal of all true believers. I went to pay him a viſit, and his taſte for drunkenneſs, which I was able to ſupply; and my zeal for in-formation, which he could alſo gratify made us more intimate.

This Effendi *, born in opulence, ſon of the Mufti, and deſtined himſelf to the Pontificate, knew no other law than his pleaſure.

Surrounded by numerous domeſtics, al-ways ready to execute his orders, he had aſſumed the property and the criminal ju-riſdiction of the village of Buyukdere; he

* Effendi, a man of the law.

had

had alfo extended his pretenfions to the
two neighbouring villages. Favours, op-
preffions, every thing there depended on
him; and the government, far from oppofing the ufurpation, by difmiffing the
complainants, added to their misfortunes
that of having made a fruitlefs complaint,
and the danger of having made any complaint at all. Another method, as effectual
of getting poffeffion of other men's property, had for a long time furnifhed Murad Mollach with the fums neceffary for
his expences, and never did man know better how to multiply them. I have known
him, while he was Kadi-lefker ‡, poffefs
nine houfes, in each of which he had a
wife, children, fervants, kitchen to feed
them, workmen building every where,
neighbours who were afraid of him, and
creditors who fled from his prefence.

‡ Kadi-lefker, this word fhould be Kadi-el-afker;
thefe three words fignify Judge of the Troops, of
whom there are two, one for Europe, and one for
Afia; this laft has the precedence of the other: they
are the two Chief Judges; every thing is fubmitted
to their decifion: In a military government there are
nothing but foldiers.

VOL. I.   E   Although

Although Murad had only the title of Mollach of Mecca ‖ when I firſt became acquainted with him, one may conceive that he was at that time in high conſideration; he was often viſited by men in office, with whom, however, he was obliged to uſe ſome precautions.

The Boſtandgy Bachi, the external officer of the Seraglio, who the moſt frequently approaches his maſter, who from his office muſt give an account of all irregularities, and who frequently takes his rounds to obſerve them, came in one of his cruizes to Buyukdere, where intending to viſit the Mollach, a ſervant of the latter informed him, that his maſter was gone to walk towards the meadow, whither the Boſtandgy Bachi went to meet him. In the interim

‖ Mollach of Mecca, is only a title peculiar to his rank, and which is preparatory to the office of Stambol Effendiſi, a ſort of Governor and Lieutenant of Police of Conſtantinople; but this office, as well as thoſe of Kadi-leſker and Mufti, does not follow in a regular rotation; arrived at the title of Kiabe Molaſſi Mollach of Mecca, the Grand Signior's choice is neceſſary, who diſpoſes of theſe places at pleaſure, provided the perſon has paſſed the third and ſecond rank before the firſt.

no time was loft to apprize the Effendi,
who was at that time at my houfe, and fo
well employed over a few bottles of Ma-
rafquino cordial, that he appeared to me
in no condition for any other bufinefs.
His fervant, however, arrives, and announces that the Boftandgy Bachi is in the neighbouring meadow.   I was devifing fome expedient to prevent any interview, the confequence of which, from the fituation he
was in, I very much dreaded ; when perceiving my fears, " You will fee," fays he
to me, fmiling, " the influence of the
mind over the body."   He fuffers his fervants, however, to fupport him to the
door of the ftreet, where he pufhes them
from him, walks fteadily, enters precipitately into the Mofque, which was only ten
paces diftant, and boldly orders them to
tell the Boftandgy Bachi he was at prayers;
from whence, a moment after, he goes to
the place where that officer waited for him,
receives his homage, difmiffes him, and returns to laugh with me at my apprehenfions on his account.

Murad Mollach, too much accuftomed
to excefs, was not eafily controuled.   He
fubmitted, however, on the reprefenta-
tions

tions I made him, to ufe fpiritous liquors
with more moderation, and confented only
to make himfelf at times a little gay.   Our
converfations became, in confequence,
more interefting.   It was from him that I
drew what I have already faid about the
women, and his women, who paid frequent vifits to Madame de Tott, very much
enriched my ftore of knowledge on that
fubject.   Being inclined to fee with my own
eyes this flock for which the fhepherd cared
but little, I once entered haftily into their
apartment: there was a general cry; it
was only the old, however, who ftrove to
hide their faces; but the vanity of the
young ones was apparent, from the flownefs with which they took that precaution.

We may fuppofe that Murad Mollach,
conftantly difgufted with the women he
already had, increafed their number from
no other motive than to procure new flaves,
whom he foon loft fight of.   I was one day
taking coffee with him in one of his kiofks,
and was endeavouring to demonftrate to
him, that fince his fyftem of predeftination did not oblige a Turk to ftay in his
houfe if it was burning, he might, with
the fame propriety, avoid the plague when
it

it broke out ; and our difpute was becom-
·ing ferious, when a little child, of about
four years old, with naked feet, and badly
clad, came to kifs his hand. The Mollach careffes him ; makes me look at the
child, and afked him who was his father ?
" You," replied he, brifkly.—" What! I
your father ? and what is your name ?"
" Jufuf." " But, who is your mother ?"
" Katidgee."---" Ah! good Katidgee!"
" Ay, indeed." Says the Effendi to me,
coldly, " I did not know him." " How,"
fays I to him, " you do not know either
your children or their mothers ? If you
are a ftranger to fuch things as thofe, what
is there which can intereft you ?"

The Mollach.

I partly agree with you ; but admit alfo,
that this mighty intereft which you reproach me with not feeling, is rather ideal.
The offspring of illufion, is it not nou-
rifhed by vanity ? Need I wifh for any
fuch refource ? No, certainly, but curiofity
is my only fentiment.

The Baron.

I believe it is alfo that of many others,
and I fhould forgive you, were it not exclufive ; but to love nothing, not even
one's

one's children, that is certainly to live in a forlorn ftate, in the moft dreadful folitude !

The Mollach.

Thefe are only high-founding words, which explain nothing, and furnifh no determinate idea. Let us be candid : All men have the fame fenfations ; their pleafures do not differ, but their prejudices, as well as their cuftoms, produce thofe varieties from which arife the moral fenfations which modify their natural ones. Let us not confound thefe. Would you think of affimilating the infignificant regulations of a fmall fociety, with the eternal laws of the Eternal Being ?

The Baron.

You are of opinion then, that, without making fo vain and abfurd a comparifon, one cannot believe in the filial fentiment ?

The Mollach.

We muft always believe in what we feel, and feel the moft we can ; but we muft not conclude that all our fenfations are fo ingrafted in our nature ; then we are wanting to her dictates in not feeling them. We have juft agreed that there are fenfations purely moral, which acting on our

our natural difpofition, controul it, and do not belong to it. We refign ourfelves to thofe fenfations, and fondly cherifh them from habit ; and perhaps they merit all that preference that is poffible. You fee that I enter into your ideas; try to enter into ours. It requires no great effort to perceive, that the eafe with which we fatisfy our inclinations produces indifference ; it is the fault of our cuftoms, we cannot change them : they procure us benefits, without employment; and employments, without benefit. Every thing is balanced :---but as long as I am curious, I fhall never be fo unhappy as you imagine.

One could eafily perceive that Murad pufhed that curiofity fometimes beyond the proper bounds; but this his metaphyfics did not attempt to juftify : he was content with making a free ufe of it.

Amongft the number of his attendants, the name of *Haidout Muftapha* had often ftruck me; the firft word fignifying *robber*, which had been, in fact, Muftapha's former trade. He ftill thought that title an honour, and his mafter ordered him to give me an account of the crimes he had committed.

committed. The narrative of a hundred heroic actions could not have been given with more noblenefs and modefty, than this rafcal affumed in recounting to us the various murders and villainies with which he was polluted. A great number of fervants, who had flocked to enjoy his narrative, joined in their applaufe ; and when he had finifhed,---" Agree with me," fays the Mollach, " that this rogue has a great deal of courage." " There is, at leaft," I anfwered, " a good deal of courage in thus braving the laws, by confefling his crimes ; and without your fupport, I fuppofe he would already have paid dearly for it." " Not at all," replied he coolly, " the law can no longer do any thing with him ; he has never fallen under its lafh whilft he exercifed his trade, and he cannot be punifhed now that he has quitted it † "

This fame fellow was afterwards employed by his mafter to look after a fort of fheep fold, together with one of his fellow fervants, who was found dead by the blow

---

† The robbers in Turkey are like unlicenfed mechanics; if they efcape the laws, and with their profits purchafe a privilege, they are free to exercife their trade ; a Pachalick in Turkey gives general licence.

of

of a hatchet, in the fame hut where they
had flept together; and Haidout Muftapha, with the utmoft effrontery, was the
firft to announce the event. He was generally looked upon as the murderer; but
the fact was too recent, no doubt, for him
to boaft of it. The Mollach, however,
who had no doubt of it, ftill continued him
in his fervice, and was conftantly attended
in his walks by this brave fellow, who
had given fuch frequent proofs of his courage.

The inconveniences of fhooting in a
country where rogues are more common
than partridges, induced me to give the
preference to fifhing, where I might hope
for more tranquillity. I frequently partook
of this diverfion, by going in a boat into a
little bay on the coaft of Afia, near the
mouth of the Black Sea, and on the other
fide of the fartheft caftles which the Turks
had then built.

Several young men were in company
with me, and we carried each of us our
gun, to amufe us on the way by fhooting
gabions §, a fort of aquatic bird, with

§. The Turkifh word is martin; a fort of fea-gull.

E 5   which

which the Canal is covered. Two boatmen, Greeks, rowed our boat, baited our
lines, and caſt our nets for us. We were
ſix ſhooters, and the birds having drawn
us acroſs the Canal, on the ſide of Aſia,
which they prefer on account of the currents, we coaſted it, and kept firing at them
from time to time. This obliged us to
paſs near the caſtle of Aſia, oppoſite to
which I knocked down a gabion. One of
the Boſtandgy's officers, who commanded
there, was ſitting ſquat at the foot of his
tower, and gravely reſpiring with the
ſmoke of his pipe, all his inſolence of office. My boatmen obſerved to me that he
made us a ſign to approach the ſhore. I
then aſked him what he wanted? " To
ſpeak to you," ſays he: " And I" ſaid I,
" have nothing to ſay to you.---I am going
to fiſh in ſuch a place; if you like the di-
verſion, come along, I will hear what you
have to ſay." The Turk then affecting
ſome reſpect for me, declared that it was
only to my boatmen he wiſhed to talk;
who, terrified at this, concluded it was to
call them to account for the ſhot I had
fired near the caſtle; but I ſoon encouraged them, by promiſing to ſtand by them;
and

and I again afked the Turk to come and fifh with us, if he was fond of the diverfion: but irritated, no doubt, at my ftile of contempt, he anfwered me very coolly, "I'll go there, and find you," and we proceeded on our expedition.

One only of the young men in company appeared uneafy at the anfwer of the Turk. Born in the country, he had imbibed with his milk a pufillanimous timidity, which ferved to divert us, by faying to him every moment, "Here come the Boftandgis!" Nobody, in fact, believed that they would really come after us, nor did we fee any fufficient reafon to induce them. We had fcarcely entered the bay, however, where we intended to fifh, before we difcovered the guard-boat coming towards us.

No alternative was now left, but to prepare for battle, which might be attended with difagreeable confequences; but we were fo remote from all affiftance, that we muft either refolve to conquer or be beaten. There was no hefitating, fo I took the command, and acted in the double capacity of foldier and politician. I firft ordered my boatmen to caft their lines and nets, that the enemy, obferving this, might fee that
we

we were not afraid of them.   I affured my
two Greeks alfo, that they had nothing
to fear, and our arms being prepared, I
gave orders to our mufketry to take aim at
the Boftandgis, as foon as I paid their officer that compliment ; but by no means to
fire before I did.   Having made this difpofition, and the Turkifh boat being already
near us, I thought it confiftent with the
European dignity to bear down upon him.
The fellow had alfo his Turkifh dignity,
and conftruing this meafure into a proof
of my fubmiffion, he left off rowing to wait
for me, which I no fooner perceived, than
I changed my manœuvre, to get at a diftance from him; and on his invitation to
continue to approach him, I anfwered that
it was his bufinefs to come after me, if he
was determined to fpeak to me. " Very
well," fays he.   My boat, however, at that
time, lay athwart the prow of his, which
was, befides, much larger.   He ordered his
people to row in fuch a manner as to fink
our boat, by ftriking us directly in the middle ; and this would infallibly have happened, had I not taken aim at him, which motion was followed by my companions, crying out at the fame time, that if he made
                                    another

another ſtroke with his oars, I would ſhoot him as I had done the gabion. The ſight alone of the end of our pieces made theſe brave fellows change their helm, and lye upon their oars. Our boats now ran along-ſide of each other, and keeping the enemy always in awe, we began our confer-ence.

At firſt I had ſome difficulty to obtain permiſſion to play the principal character; for the Turk whom I had juſt humbled, ſaid to the boatmen, " that Frank does not un-derſtand me; do you ſpeak." One muſt be acquainted with the crouching meanneſs of a Greek towards a Turk, to judge of the degree of inſolence my boatmen ven-tured to diſplay in anſwering the officer, " that I ſpoke the Turkiſh language better than he did;" and he was at length forced to addreſs himſelf to me.

TURK.

Has Conſtantinople then paſſed under the yoke of the Infidels? By what right do you preſume to oppoſe the guard which looks after the ſafety and good order of the Canal?

EURO-

EUROPEAN.

And by what right do you prefume yourfelf, to violate the engagements of your
mafter, by molefting his beft friends?

TURK.

I do not moleft you; but it is forbid to
fhoot here without permiffion: fhew me
your authority.

EUROPEAN.

Where did you fee any body fhoot hares
in a boat? I am fifhing, and the fifhery is
free.

TURK.

No, nothing is free here, not even the
walks, and I have a long firman †, to which
you muft fubmit.

EUROPEAN.

Yes, when I have feen it.

TURK.

You cannot read.

EUROPEAN.

Better than you; but I fee that you
have none. You are a fellow who make
ufe of falfe pretences: we are ftrictly in
order.

† An order iffued from the Porte in the name of
the Grand Signior.

TURK.

TURK.

How! Have you not fired a fhot oppofite the Imperial fortrefs?

EUROPEAN.

Before *you*, I admit that I have fired;
but before a fortrefs, that is impoffible,
without you beftow that name on an old
pigeon-houfe you were fitting under. This
was furely not a very refpectable object,
and I will make you repent your infolence.
The Boftandgy Bachi is my friend, and I
fhall defire him to beftow a hundred ftrokes
of his ftick upon you, before my door, by
way of amufing myfelf.

TURK.

Why are you out of humour? Have I
done you any harm?

EUROPEAN.

No; thanks to my gun, which fright-
ened you.

TURK.

Cannot one enter into an explanation
with you, without your being in a paffion?
As for me, I am not out of humour; I am
your friend, treat me in the fame manner,
and amufe yourfelf.

EURO-

EUROPEAN.

Oh! I underſtand you ; a dollar would be very acceptable, but you ſhall not have it.

TURK.

What, nothing!

EUROPEAN.

No ; nothing but the rain, which will certainly wet you if you don't make haſte and get to your pigeon houſe.   Adieu!

This adventure, which terminated by the retreat of the aſſailants in the ſight of ſeveral Turkiſh fiſhermen acquainted with that coaſt procured us from them the moſt favourable reception ; and we found them on landing much more attentive than uſual. I did not fail, on my return, to make my complaint to the Boſtandgy Bachi, who gave him orders to aſk my pardon, and we became very good friends.

There was this year, at Conſtantinople, one of thoſe winds ſo formidable through-out all Aſia, which the Turks call *cham yiely*, the damaſk wind ; it blows mode-rately from ſouth ſouth eaſt, but loads the atmoſphere with an earthy fog, which darkens the air, and contributes, no doubt, by that, more than by its exceſſive heat, to

ſuffocate

fuffocate the travellers and country people who are unacquainted with the method of preferving themfelves, by breathing from time to time with their mouths againſt the ground; even in the houfes one is very much incommoded by it; and for three days that this wind continued, I was under the neceſſity of placing my mouth often againſt the wall, in order to refpire more freely.

Excepting this wind, which very feldom blows, the climate of Conſtantinople adds much to the beauty of its fituation. They have fcarcely any other than foutherly and northerly winds, which fucceed each other, and often claſh together at the point of the Seraglio. The latter are generally trade winds in fummer, that die away at the fetting of the fun, and begin to blow at about ten in the morning, and during the great heats, much later. The foutherly winds prevail generally in winter, and regularly follow the fnow ſtorms from the northward, and which they very quickly melt. It is obferved, however, that the firſt day of the foutherly wind after the fnow, conveys a very ſharp cold to Conſtantinople, and produces the hardeſt froſts;

it

it then becomes more mild, makes a thaw, and is productive fometimes of the greateft heats.

The fituation of Mount Olympus, which is conftantly covered with fnow, is the caufe and explanation of this phenomenon. This lofty mountain, at the foot of which is built the ancient town of Prufa *, is fituated in Afia, in fight, and in the meridian of Conftantinople. The frefh fnows that are carried there by the northerly winds, produce an exceffive cold, which the firft blaft of the foutherly wind conveys to Conftantinople ; and it is not till the atmofphere is cleared of that frozen air, that it refumes its characteriftic mildnefs. The pofition of that city renders it alfo very liable to frequent ftorms, which are followed by a rapid brightnefs in the north-weft, and the wind from that quarter very foon piles up the clouds in heaps over Afia Minor. This is at leaft the picture of the heavens in this country, as they commonly appear. The northerly breezes, by refrefhing the Canal, add to the beauty of the different fituations on its borders

* A town built by Hannibal.

on the two coafts of Afia and of Europe,
which attract all the great men of the empire, who repair there in 'fummer to their
country-houfes; and as the moft beautiful fituations are occupied by the Grand
Signior, or laid out in walks, thefe palaces
ferve to decorate the Canal. They alfo
afford profpects fo much the more agreeable, as that nature is no where fatigued
by ftraight line plantations, cropt arbours,
and maffes of ftone, that fubftitute a burning fandy terrace, for the natural and frefh
lawns to which the Turks give the preference.

It is perhaps neither owing to want of
art, nor to good tafte, which fets a proper
value on fimplicity, that we muft attribute the pains taken by the Turks to preferve nature, in order to enjoy it in its primitive ftate. They are particularly fond
of the fhade of large trees, and facrifice
even the plan of their houfes to their prefervation. I have feen a houfe where the
architect had preferved a handfome elm of
longer ftanding than the proprietor, in the
midft of a gallery, through which it was
fuffered to pierce, for no other purpofe
than to fhade the roof. All the trees on the
ground

ground are preferved, in what manner fo-
ever they happen to be placed; and, in
general, the plan of the building is governed by them, and this, no doubt, becaufe in a hot climate the fhade of large
trees is neceffary. Under a defpotic government, a man muft enjoy the trees that
he can find; he has not the time to fee them
grow up.

Hanum Sultana, the Grand Signior's
niece, had a handfome palace on the Canal,
where fhe paffed the fummer; her uncle,
Sultan Ofman, often went to fee her, and
that Princefs had fo much influence over
him, as to furnifh matter for fcandal. Still
young, yet long fince married, fhe had
fcarcely known her hufband, who had
been appointed to a Pachalick fhortly after
his marriage. The intereft of the different Vifirs kept him at a diftance, the laws
did not allow the Sultana to go to him,
and the fentiment the uncle had for the
niece, was not calculated to bring the couple together.

The manner in which the word Sultana
is abufed in Europe, induces me to make
fome obfervations, which will ferve, I hope,
to rectify every error on that head.

This

The word *Sultan*, is only a title of birth appropriated to the Ottoman Princes, born on the throne, and to thofe of the Gengif-kan family. This word, which is pronounced *Soultan*, is, without doubt, alfo the true etymology of *Soudan*; and this title in Egypt is fynonimous with that of a *King*; but neither in Turkey, nor Tartary, does it imply any idea of fove-reign authority. The title of *Kam* is peculiarly attached to the Sovereign of the Tartars, and is equivalent to that of *Chach*, fignifying *King*, with the Perfians, from whence is derived *Padi Chach*, *Great King*, which the Ottoman family has affumed, either for the purpofe of refufing or granting it to different powers, who have not perceived, perhaps, that there would have been more addrefs and dignity in not acknowledging, than in claiming this title. That of Sultan gives its poffeffors the capacity of fucceeding to the throne, and the eftablifhed order of fucceffion amongft the Turks is always in the oldeft of the family, who muft, as I have already faid, be born on the throne.

Sultan Mahamout dying without iffue, after a reign of one and twenty years, left
the

the empire to his brother Ofman, the eldeft
of four remaining fons of Sultan Achmet,
who was dethroned by a revolution. Muftapha, who fucceeded Ofman, Bajazet who
died in the Seraglio, and Abdul Amid, the
reigning Sultan, were about the fame age
with Ofman, who leaving no pofterity, his
family was threatened with deftruction, had
his reign lafted as long as it might have
done ; but it was only of three years duration, and Sultan Muftapha very foon gave
two heirs to the empire, one of whom is
now living in the perfon of Sultan Selim,
who was fhut up after the death of his father, but deftined to fucceed his uncle, Abdul Amid, to the exclufion of his living and
unborn coufins. It is to be hoped that this
Prince, ftill young, will mount the throne
at an age capable of enfuring the continuance of the dynafty of the Ottoman
Princes, to which this order of fucceffion
has frequently threatened to put an end, an
event fufficient alfo to annihilate the empire, to the poffeffion of which no law gives
any claim to the Gengifkan race. This
prejudice, which has gained credit, has induced me to inform myfelf of its truth
from the Kam of the Tartars, and that
Prince

Prince has affured me, that it has no foundation. It may be prefumed, however, that in cafe of the extinction of the Ottoman family, the factions which would tear in pieces its inheritance, muft decide the men of the law to call one of the Sultan Tartars to the throne, for want of the collateral branches, which the feeblenefs of the defpot, armed with the moft atrocious barbarity, has cut off at their birth.

I do not, however, fpeak of thofe branches which may fpring from the Princes fhut up by policy in the interior of the Seraglio, and who are allowed to have wives; their children born between the throne and the ftate, would neither belong to the one nor the other. A falfehood may likewife fpare nature the horror of knowing they are deftroyed, and prejudice may ftill further propagate the flattering error, that the wives of thefe Princes are no longer of an age to render the crime neceffary.

But the daughters and fifters of the Grand Signior, married to the Vifirs and great men of the empire, live feparately in the palaces, and the male infant of the marriage muft be fmothered at the fame moment, and by the fame hands that bring

it

it into the world. This is at once the moſt public and moſt inviolable law, no veil is thrown over the horror of theſe murders. A cowardly fear produces theſe aſſaſſinations, more than the real intereſt of the throne. What advantages of ſituation can conſole theſe unhappy Princeſſes ?——But what freſh horror! The pride of their birth, which compels this crime, more monſtrous than the crime itſelf, not ſatisfied with the victim, ſmothers even the cry of nature.

If the female children alone eſcape this murderous law, they are obliged to add to the title of Sultana, that of Hanum, a title common to all women of eaſy fortune; and the children of both ſexes which theſe Princeſſes are able to preſerve, return in the next generation into the general claſs: they bear no longer any title of diſtinction. Deſcended from a grand daughter of the Grand Signior, they are already ſtript of all the influence of paternal ſentiments. The great grandfather has already loſt ſight of them in the obſcurity of their birth.

Such is the rule of eſtabliſhing the rank of Sultana amongſt the Turks. The Tartars, more humane, becauſe they are not deſpotic, defpotic, fmother nobody: they content themfelves with making the Sultana's fon adopt the name, the rank, and titles of the Mirza whom fhe has chofen to be its father.

That female flave of the Seraglio, who becomes the mother of a Sultan, and who may live long enough to fee her fon mount upon the Throne, is alfo the only woman who can, at that period alone, acquire without the advantage of birth, the diftinction of *Sultana valide, Sultana mother.*

Maintained until then in the interior of her prifon, with her fon, fhe muft be contented only to poffefs the efteem which he may have for her. It is evident that the title of *favourite Sultana* is the more abfurd; for that, if fhe be the Sultana, fhe cannot avow that fort of preference; and the moment fhe can poffefs it, fhe is no longer Sultana.

The title of *Bache Kadun*, principal woman, is the firft dignity of the Grand Signior's harem: fhe has a larger allowance than thofe who have the title of fecond, third, and fourth woman; but thefe advantages do not always indicate the real favourite. The reigning Grand Signior had confecrated thefe diftinctions to his grati-

Vol. I.   F   tude,

tude, by beftowing them on women who had partaken of his retirement. He can difpofe of them at his pleafure, by confining thofe who already poffefs them in the old Seraglio. None of thefe four women are married to him : they reprefent only the four free women which the law allows. One may prefume alfo, that they are there only for fhow.

I have already faid, that the difficulty of accefs to the Grand Signior's harem, where only a few doctors are admitted, and that, after removing every thing but what is connected with the diforder, leaves no other method of judging of it than from the knowledge of the cuftoms which prevail in the harems of individuals.

The Palace even of a Sultana, where every thing, even to her hufband, is at her command, can give no infight into what paffes in the Seraglio. I do not pretend, therefore, to caft a ray of light into that truly inacceffible dungeon; nor am I going to offer any objects of comparifon; I fhall confine myfelf to fimple details, which ought to be deemed curious; they give at leaft a picture of manners, and I am happy in fatisfying, in this refpect, the anxiety of
the

the public, by defcribing, as Madame de
Tott dictates to me, a vifit fhe made with
her mother to Sultana Afma, daughter of
the Emperor Achmet, and fifter to his fucceffors to this day.

Under the reign of Sultan Mahamout,
this Princefs ftill young and prejudiced by
the example of her brother in favour of the
Franks, was defirous of converfing with
an European woman. My mother-in-law,
although born in Turkey, anfwered the
purpofe of her curiofity, and was invited
to wait on her with her daughter. The
female attendant of the exterior of the Palace, was directed to receive, and conduct
them to the Sultana. On their arrival at
the Seraglio of that Princefs, (the fame as
I have already faid that the Vifir was lodged in after the fire) the conductrefs made
them enter by a firft and fecond iron gate,
guarded by different porters; but who were
in no way different from the ordinary race
of men, any more than the guardian of the
third gate, which opening all at the command of the intendante, difcovered feveral
black eunuchs, who, with white ftaves in
their hands, preceded the female ftrangers

F 2   through

through an inner court, entrufted to their keeping, and introduced them into a large room called the ftranger's chamber.

The Kiaya Cadun, or Intendante of the interior apartments of the Seraglio, came to do the honours, and the flaves fhe had brought affifted the two ftrangers to un-mafk and fold up their veils, whilft their miftrefs went to acquaint the Sultana with their arrival. The Princefs, however, de-voted to the prejudices of her religion, would only receive the vifit from behind the blinds, that fhe might fee, without being feen; but my mother-in-law declaring fhe would withdraw if the Sultana perfifted in concealing herfelf, the negociation was ter-minated by the confent of the Princefs, who contrived time to think of her drefs, by in-viting my mother to reft herfelf a little be-fore fhe came up to her apartment. Con-ducted accordingly foon after by the In-tendante and a great number of flaves, they found the Sultana, on entering her apartments, richly dreffed, and fet off with all her diamonds, feated in a corner of a rich fopha that furnifhed her faloon, the ta-peftry peſtry * and carpets of which were of gold and ſilver lyons ſtuff, ſewn together in breadths of different colours. The *feliƈtes* †, covered with ſattin, ſtriped with gold, carried and ſpread before the Sultana, ſerved for them to ſit on ; whilſt ſixty young girls, richly clad, and in looſe robes, divided themſelves on the right and left at the entrance of the hall, forming two rows with their hands croſſed on their waiſts.

After the firſt compliments, the Princeſs's queſtions turned upon the liberty enjoyed by our women. She compared it with the cuſtoms of the harem, and ſhowed ſome difficulty in conceiving, how the face of a young girl could be viewed before marriage by her future huſband. But, theſe different queſtions diſcuſſed, ſhe concurred in the advantages reſulting from our cuſtoms, and giving looſe to the natu-

---

* The Turks are very little acquainted with this kind of luxury, which is only to be found within the harems, where a kind of curtain extends behind the cuſhions, and covers the wall half way up: but the hall of the throne, which has no ſopha, is entirely covered with tapeſtry.

† Seliƈtes is a ſmall cotton mattreſs, covered with ſtuff.

ral

ral fenfations arifing from her own perfonal fituation, fhe exclaimed againft the barbarity of the inftitution, which, at thirteen years old, had put her in the power of a decrepid old man, who, by treating her like a child, had only infpired her with difguft. *He died, however, at laft*, added fhe; *but am I more happy?* "Ten years have I been married to a young Pacha, who, they fay, is young and amiable, but we have never feen each other."

The Princefs then faid many polite things to the two European ladies, and gave orders to her Intendante to treat them handfomely; and after taking a walk, to provide an entertainment for them in the garden, and to re-conduct them to her to conclude the vifit.

The Intendante led them accordingly to her apartments, where they dined alone with her; whilft a number of flaves, forming a row around the table, were wholly employed in ferving them.

The dinner finifhed, and the coffee ferved, the European ladies were offered pipes, which they refufed, and which the Intendante hardly gave herfelf time to finifh, before fhe conducted her guofts into the

the garden, where fresh bands of flaves were arranged near a very beautiful kiofk, the place where the company were to af-femble.

This pavillion, richly furnifhed and or-namented, built over a large bafon of wa-ter, occupied the middle of the garden, where efpaliers of rofes, rifing on all fides, concealed from the eye the lofty walls that formed this prifon. Small foot paths, very narrow, and paved with mofaic, were, ac-cording to cuftom, the only walks in the garden; but a great number of pots, and bafkets of flowers, prefented to the eye a little clufter, beautifully coloured, invited the fenfes to partake of their fweets in the corner of a good fopha, the only object of this fort of walks. They were fcarcely feated, before the eunuchs, who had head-ed the proceffion, ranged themfelves in a row at fome diftance from the kiofk, to give room for the Princefs's band of mufic, confifting of ten women flaves, who per-formed different pieces; during which a troop of women dancers, as richly, but more loofely dreffed, executed feveral bal-lets that were tolerably agreeable both for the variety of fteps and figures. Thefe
women

women dancers were alfo of a higher clafs
than they ufually are in private houfes.
Soon after arrived a frefh troop of women,
dreffed like men, to add, no doubt, to this
picture, the illufion of a fex which was
wanting to the entertainment.   Thefe pretended men began a fort of tilting on the
water, to win the fruits which other flaves
threw into the bafon.   The ftrangers had
alfo the pleafure of going on the water in a
fmall boat, rowed by female rowers, difguifed alfo like men ; after which being
led back to the Sultana's apartment, they
took leave of her with the ufual ceremonies, and were conducted out of the Seraglio
by the fame paffage, and in the fame order
by which they were introduced.

It appears from this defcription, that the
Eunuchs were more at the command of the
Sultana than difpofed to thwart her. Thefe
beings are no other than an object of luxury
in Turkey, difplayed no where but in the
Seraglios of the Grand Signior, and the Sultanas. The pride of the great, 'tis true, extends fo far, but with moderation, and the
richeft of them have fcarcely ever more than
two or three black Eunuchs. The white
ones, who are lefs deformed, are referved for
                                                    the

the Grand Signior, to form the guard for
the outer-gates of his Seraglio; but they are
not fuffered to approach the women, nor
obtain any employment, whilft the poffibility of arriving at the poft of Kiflar Aga,
furnifhes the black Eunuchs, at leaft, a
motive to fupport and animate their ambition.   Their character is always ferocious,
and nature offended in their perfons, feems
perpetually to feel the reproach.

Although the feaft of Tchiragan *, an
entertainment the Grand Signior often
takes, cannot enable one to form any judgment of the infide of the Seraglio, the particulars of it may appear interefting, by
giving fome idea of his pleafures †.

The garden of the Harem, larger, no
doubt, than that of Sultana Afma, but laid
out certainly in the fame tafte, ferves as
the theatre of thefe nocturnal feafts. Vafes
of every kind, filled with natural or artifi-
cial flowers, are gathered there to augment

* The Feaft of Tulips; which is fo called, becaufe
it confifts in illuminating a Parterre; and that this is
the flower of which the Turks are the fondeft.

† One may be apt to imagine, that thofe which
he habitually takes, are lefs lively than thofe he procures himfelf, in illuminating his tulips.

the

the clufter, which is lighted by an infinite
number of lanthorns, coloured lamps, and
wax lights, placed in glafs tubes, and reflected by looking glafſes, difpofed for that
purpofe. Temporary fhops, filled with
different forts of merchandize, are occupied by women of the Harem, who reprefent, in fuitable drefſes, the merchants
who might be fuppofed to fell them. The
Sultanas, who are the fifters, nieces, or
coufins of the Grand Signior are invited to
thefe entertainments, and they, as well as
his Highnefs, purchafe trinkets and ftuffs
in thefe fhops, which they mutually make
prefents of to one another; they extend
their generofity alfo to fuch of the Grand
Signior's women as are admitted to approach him, or who keep the fhops.—
Dancing, mufic, and fports fimilar to the
tilting on the water I have fpoken of, pro-
long thefe entertainments until the night
is far advanced, and diffufe a fort of momentary gaiety within thefe walls, generally devoted to forrow, and to dulnefs. It
is alfo from Madame de Tott that I obtained thefe relations, which fhe received
from the Sultana Hanum, of whom, as I
have

have already faid, her uncle was very
fond.

My brother-in-law had become very intimate with the Intendante of that Princefs,
in order to obtain her intereft in favour of
his friends, or for his own concerns. The
chief of her Eunuchs was alfo well difpofed
towards him ; the Sultana had feen him
feveral times through her window-blinds;
he had a handfome face, and every thing
combined to procure him her good wifhes.
Deprived for a long time of her hufband,
by whom fhe had a fon and a daughter, the
Princefs feemed to endeavour to confole
herfelf in his abfence, and to have availed
herfelf of that want of rank, which approach
her condition to that of ordinary individuals, by adopting their manners. In fact,
one faw that jealoufy which reigns amongft
the Turkifh women difplay itfelf in lively
colours around her perfon. The pains fhe
took in dreffing Madame de Tott's hair,
whom fhe had defired to fee, difpleafed the
woman who was her principal favourite fo
much, as to make her faint away ; and
Madame de Tott returned home more
ftruck with the particular marks of affection
the Sultana had lavifhed on her, than with
the

the exceſſive magnificence that reigned in her palace, and amongſt her ſlaves.

The Patriarch Kirlo, filled at that time, the œcumenical chair of Conſtantinople ; this man, born of the dregs of the people, amongſt whom his fanaticiſm had ſucceeded in forming a party, made himſelf feared by the firſt people of his nation, whoſe pride, in other reſpects, held him in contempt.

Aided by ſome members of the Synod, he imagined and maintained the doctrine of baptiſm by immerſion : the anathema that he pronounced on this ſubject from his metropolis, againſt the Pope, the King of France, and all the Catholic Princes, determined his flock to renew their baptiſm ; and the women, and young girls, always devotees, crouded to that holy ceremony, which ſcandal converted into a crime againſt the Apoſtle and his proſelytes.

Beſides the inſolence of an excommunication, which could have no other object than the inſult, this Patriarch, conſtantly employed in feeding the fanaticiſm of his nation, paid the Turks a recompenſe for the vexations with which he harraſſed the Catholics ; he even extended his oppreſſi-
ons

ons to fuch bifhops of his church as had
the courage not to be fubfervient to his
projects, and he perfecuted thefe unfortunate defpotis with the moft unrelenting barbarity, after having ftript them of their
temporal poffeffions. Of this number was
Kalinico, Archbifhop of Amafia. He had
taken refuge in our quarter, to avoid the
fentence which confined him to Mount Sinai, and folicited the intereft of my brother-in-law with Sultana Hanum, to obtain
from the Grand Signior the reftitution of
his Archbifhoprick. This would certainly
have been a very good work, but it would
not probably have excited anxiety in favour
of the Prelate, had not the defire of banifh-
ing Kirlo, tempted us to convert his victim
into his rival. Whilft my brother-in-law
negotiated this affair, by the mediation
and influence of Sultana Hanum, with the
Grand Signior, fome perfons hired by the
Patriarch to carry off Kalinico, attempted
to feize him one night near my houfe,
where he had barely time to take refuge.
To enfure at once, therefore, the fafety of
his perfon, and to place him in readinefs
for his affairs, I confented to let him ftay
in a kiofk built on the roof of my houfe,
where

where I fecretly took care of him, and fed him, until his elevation to the Patriarchate, for which my brother-in-law bargained a long time, and at length obtained, for a pretty confiderable fpecific fum, to be paid in new fequins *.

The *Katti Cherif* † of the Grand Signior, which depofed Kirlo, and gave him Kalinico for a fucceffor, reached the Vifir before that Minifter had the fmalleft fufpicion of what was plotting. To juftify this fudden degradation, the order was conceived in very ftrong terms, and imputed to the Patriarch a turbulent fpirit, difpofed to a revolt, and concluded with an injunction to take the moft efficacious meafures to apprehend his perfon, and prevent his efcape by flight from Mount Sinai, to which place the fame order reftricted him. The Minifters of the Porte, however, took mea-

---

* It was the Grand Signior himfelf who required that claufe, which could not be fulfilled without having recourfe to the mint; and the fum paffed directly from the fcales into the hands of Sultan Ofman, who fhared it with his niece.

† Katti Cherif, Imperial Signet, or Diploma;— which has the force of law, and muft be executed without a demur.

fures

fures to ward off the imaginary danger,
which their pufillanimity fuggefted to be
very urgent. Some companies of Janiſſaries had orders early in the morning, to
take poffeffion of all the avenues of the
Greek quarter; the guards were doubled
in the environs, and the Patriarchal palace,
ftill more carefully furrounded, delivered
up Kirlo to his conquerors, without any re-
fiſtance. They conveyed him without de-
lay to a coal-boat, where they depoſited
him. Excepting this circumſtance, which
did not ennoble the fcene, never was there
a Greek for whom it was lefs neceſſary to
take thofe precautions that illuſtrated his
fall; and his countrymen were fo far from
thinking of refcuing him from the Grand
Signior's orders, that had it not been for
the triviàl circumſtance of the coal-boat,
even their vanity would have been gratified.

It now remained only for the Porte to
inftall his fucceſſor ; and the government
would not have known where to find him,
had not the Grand Signior, acquainted with
the whole affair, pointed out the place.
Some of the Vifir's people, difpatched immediately, came to afk for him at my houfe,

to

to conduct him to the Porte ; and this poor despoti *, more accustomed to fear than hope, was begging me not to deliver him up to his enemies, when I announced to him his elevation ; I could not, however, quiet his apprehensions; but, forced to obey, he followed his guides, whom he took to be executioners, and in an hour after was proclaimed Patriarch.

I received a message of thanks from him the same day, and he came afterwards to visit me in his good fortune, to desire me always to reserve for him his place of retreat, which he believed he should stand in need of very shortly. I then perceived that we had made but an indifferent choice of a Patriarch for the Primitive church.

It furnished me, however, with a favourable opportunity of assisting at the ceremonies preserved by the Greek church, and I attended one great holy day at the Metropolitan ; some of the new Patriarch's attendants waited for me, and placed me, by his order, in a stall at the right of his seat,

* A title which the Greek Bishops have assumed to mark the absolute power they possess ; but of which the Grand Signior makes them feel the proper application.

where

where he foon placed himfelf; and every
thing being prepared for beginning the fervice, he defcended from thence, and feated himfelf in a chair, carried for that purpofe, oppofite the *facra fanctorum*. There,
feveral Deacons proceeded to inveft him
with his pontifical robes, and at length put
on his head a clofe crown of diamonds, with
a double crofs upon the globe.

The Patriarch then took the patriarchal
ftaff in his left hand, and in his right a
fmall wax taper, of three branches, of which
he only held two, to mark the union of the
Father and the Son, without adding the
Holy Ghoft. He obferved the fame form
by bending the middle fingers of his hand
when he gave the benediction, by which
means the Holy Ghoft fignified by the little finger, remained feparated from the Son,
from whom the Greeks do not believe that
it proceeds.

The Patriarch was then introduced into
the fanctuary, the curtain of which was
fhut, and the people who crouded the
church, and had till then obferved a tolerably refpectful filence, began to be agi-
tated in as tumultuous a manner as the
waves of the Parterre at our public thea-
tres

tres in France ; but the indecent burfts of laughter occafioned by this agitation, were very foon confounded with the cries of the unhappy wretches in danger of fuffocation. One of thefe, after having been for fome time trodden under foot, was lifted up before me over the people's heads, which were fo clofely jammed together, that, with the affiftance of fome hands that raifed him up, and pufhed him backwards, he reached the bottom of the church, where they fent him to recover his breath in that very extraordinary manner.

This fcene, which I viewed without danger from the height of my ftall, by ruffling a few ears, increafed the noife to fuch a degree, that the Patriarch brifkly opening the curtain that concealed him from the people, harangued them in a difcourfe as violent as the noife which had occafioned it ; and he finifhed this paftoral exhortation by *fending his flock to the Devil.* But the calm which fucceeded that harangue was of fhort duration, and the moment of the facrifice approaching, it was neceffary to have recourfe to a more efficacious method than the eloquence of the Pontiff. It was by very heavy ftrokes of his cane that the

Patriarch's

Patriarch's Janiffary recalled the affembly to the attention due to the holy myftery then about to be expofed to them. The lateral doors of the *facra fanctorum* were now thrown open, and the Deacons came out with all the inftruments of the Greek Liturgy, to offer them fucceffively at the middle gate, where they announced one after the other, and with a loud voice, each of the inftruments they carried. The Patriarchal crown, which finifhed the proceffion, was alone refufed ; and this teftimony of the contempt of riches, borrowed from the holy Evangelifts, and the facred veffels, added, no doubt, to the marks of refpect that the Patriarch had juft given.

The fucceeding ceremonies of the fervice had nothing remarkable in them. I accompanied the Patriarch home, and he kept me to dinner. I took the opportunity, likewife, of my vifit to the *Fanal*, or Greek quarter, to wait upon the Drogman of the Porte, whofe family, particularly attached to Madame de Tott, had made her promife to pafs a few days at their country houfe on the Canal. Amongft the number of

of Archontes * whom I met with at the
houfe of this interpreter of the Grand Signior, Manoly Serdar †, faithfully attached
to the fate of Racovitza, the depofed Prince
of Wallachia, appeared to me to poffefs
more ability and information than his countrymen. He won my efteem by that difin-
terefted zeal which made him prefer medi-
ocrity with his former benefactor, to thofe
advantages his ingratitude might have procured him in the fervice of the new Princes.
No temptation had been able to fhake his
fidelity, and the reftoration of Racovitza
was the fole object of all his meafures. It
was undoubtedly with this view, and from
the opinion the elevation of Kalinico had
given him of the influence of my brother-
in-law, that Manoly Serdar, defirous of a
greater intimacy with him, wifhed alfo to
connect himfelf with me, as earneftly as I
did, to be acquainted with a man fo capable of inftructing me in the character and
manners of his nation. We became more
intimate in the country, where this Greek
came to live near me. We were never fe-

* A title which the opulent Greeks ftill affume.

† Serdar, a Turkifh word, Governor.

parate;

parate; and I heard him with pleafure frequently declare, that his nation preferved
no other trace of the character of the ancient empire of the Greeks than the pride and
fanaticifm that produced its downfall. Manoly Serdar, however, had nothing left to
live on but the capital he had amaffed during the time that Prince Racovitza poffeffed the principality of Wallachia, and I
faw, with regret, that the luxury of his
wife, and the great number of his flaves,
combined together to expofe his virtue to
the temptations of neceffity, whilft his
vanity banifhed every fuggeftion of œconomy.

The ftile of familiarity in which we
lived, enabled me to form an idea of his
domeftic life; and I there daily difcovered
a mixture of Greek and Turkifh manners.
A little lamp conftantly burning before the
picture of the Panaghia *, lighted at the
fame time the young flaves who dreffed,
and undreffed the Serdar : this Greek, as
well as all thofe who are in fuch eafy circumftances as to introduce at their houfes
the Turkifh fervice, had alfo the cuftom of

---

* The Virgin.

fleeping

sleeping on his sopha after dinner, whilst a
woman, by driving away the flies with a
large fan of feathers, cooled the air that he
was respiring. Other slaves kneeling at
his naked feet, rubbed them gently with
their hands. This Asiatic effeminacy
gives room to suspect, that these refine-
ments are carried to greater lengths, and
the ill treatment bestowed by this Greek
on his slaves for the slightest faults, only
proves, that where the facility of enjoyment is without bounds, there is an end to
delicacy.

I was at length obliged to fulfill the pro-
mise, made by Madame de Tott, to the
lady of the chief Drogman, to pass some
days with her. We went to her country-
house : the family consisted of the old
Drogman, whose professional knowledge
compensated for his dulness and gross ig--
norance ; but whose knowledge of foreign
language was limited to a little bad Italian.
His wife, who was not so far advanced in
years, and who had substituted an air of
Majesty in the place of beauty, had the
internal management of his house, of
which she did the honours with a sort of
frank cordiality, which slightly concealed
the

the pride of knowing herfelf to be, in virtue of her hufband's office, the firft perfon
of her nation.

The eldeft of her fons, whom we fhall
fee fucceed his father in the principality of
Moldavia, to make an unhappy end, was
of a character naturally mild, but weak and
vain; the younger, of a more haughty
character, already announced that intrigu-
ing and ambitious fpirit which coft his brother his life : an eldeft daughter, a widow
at nineteen, frefher than the morning rofe,
elegantly flender without being tall, united
to the moft bewitching graces, a certain
modefty, a fweetnefs, and a languid air
which were irrefiftable : the younger fifter
lefs beautiful, but lively and interefting,
was juft betrothed to a young Greek in the
neighbourhood. The intended hufband
was anxious, no doubt, to become acquainted with us, and we were but juft
arrived when two or three flaves came to
announce him, by entering precipitately
in the faloon, where the family was affembled ; they throw themfelves on the
betrothed girl, cover her with their robes,
and carry her off, crying out, like mad
people, " get out of the way, there he is."

In

In fact, we faw the young man enter,
who, although careffed by the whole family, could never caft his eyes on the object of his defire, but by furprize. He
had often tried the fame experiment, but
always without fuccefs. They kept him to
fupper, and the young girl was kept out of
fight until his departure.

The hour of withdrawing being come,
we were conducted into a fpacious adjoining apartment, in the middle of which
was a bed, without bedftead or curtains,
but the coverlet and pillows furpaffed in
magnificence the richnefs of the fopha
which decorated the apartment. I had
but little profpect of repofe on this bed,
and was curious to examine it minutely.
Fifteen quilted cotton mattreffes, about
three inches thick, laid one upon another,
formed a very foft foundation, covered by
a fheet of Indian linen tacked to the laft
mattrefs. A counterpane of green fattin,
loaded with gold wire embroidery; emboffed, was alfo faftened to the upper fheet,
the edges of which were turned up and
ftitched together. Two large pillows of
crimfon fattin, covered with fimilar embroidery, in which gold plating and twifted
gold

gold thread were profufely lavifhed, were
fupported by two cufhions of the fopha,
brought near to ferve by way of a back-
board, and alfo to fupport our heads. A
fmall octagon tower, inlaid with ebony and
mother of pearl, formed a fort of table at
the fide of the bed, on which was placed
a large filver candleftick, with a yellow
wax taper, two inches thick, the wick of
which as large as one's finger, fpread a
black fmoke. Three China falvers, filled
with conferve of rofes, orange flowers, and
citron peeling ; a fmall gold knife, with a
tortoife fhell handle, and a cryftal vafe full
of water, furrounded this obfcure lumina-
ry, which was to ferve us as a night lamp;
a precaution abfolutely neceffary every
where from the proximity of the neighbouring houfes, which give conftant reafon to apprehend the fatal ravages of fire.
The Drogman's houfe was precifely in this
fituation, and every thing prepared me for
a bad night's reft. The fuppreffion of the
pillows would have been of fome fervice,
had there been a bolfter ; and the expedient of turning them having ferved only to
difcover the embroidery below, we were at
length obliged to fpread our handkerchiefs

VOL. I.   -   G   over

over them, which did not fecure us, however, from the impreffion of the emboffed
flowers.   After fuch a night we were not
very lazy in rifing; and we faw, with joy,
the day break, with a determination of
procuring more convenient pillows for the
following night.

A fifhing party propofed the night before, preceded our breakfaft, which was
carried over to Afia, where a fmall meadow, a Turkifh coffee-houfe, and fome
loaded carts, drawn by little buffalos, gave
the ladies the profpect of every thing agreeable that the country afforded.   Our fuccefs in fifhing was indifferent; the ladies
were well jolted, and the Turkifh women
in company were very troublefome with
their queftions, and very infolent in their
anfwers.   We brought back with us fome
jars filled with curds, and fome creffes gathered at a fountain; and there was but one
opinion on the fubject of the pleafures we
had juft been enjoying.

We found at our return to the Drogman's, feveral Greek women of the neighbourhood, who were invited to dinner, and
were already affembled.   A fplendid drefs,
in which vanity was evidently more con-
fulted

fulted than the feafon, was difplayed on a grand fopha, in robes of black, or crimfon velvet, covered with broad gold lace on all the feams. The weight of thefe garments, joined to the heat of the weather, rendered thefe ladies immoveable, and almoft mute. They held, however, a common-place converfation, with frequent repetitions of the fame thing, and the company went to table. Dinner was ferved in the French ftile; a circular table, with chairs round it, fpoons and forks; in fhort, nothing was wanting but the habit of making ufe of them. They were defirous, notwithftanding, of not negleɗing any part of our cuftoms, which began to be as much in fafhion amongft the Greeks, as the Englifh cuftoms are in France; and I have feen a woman after dinner, take the olives in her fingers, and prick them with her fork, to eat them *a la Françaife.* If drinking healths is no longer in fafhion with us, it is not the lefs agreeable to meet with this ancient cuftom in other countries. Our Greeks were not wanting in this refpeɗ; and the men performed the ceremony ftanding up, uncovered. But what will appear fomewhat lefs refined, the fame

wine-

wine-glafs ferved the whole company. After the dinner, where profufion was difplayed, more than elegance or neatnefs,
the company arranged themfelves on the
fopha, in the fame room where we had
dined, and pipes fucceeded the coffee.
The converfation began on the fafhions,
and finifhed with fcandal ; the trueft imitation of our manners that I ever faw in
that country. The young girls amufed
themfelves in the mean time with a fwing,
fufpended at the other end of the room,
and put in motion by the flaves. The women likewife partook of that amufement,
and were followed by the men with long
beards ; and the tout de table, chefs, and
panguelo, a kind of brelan, finifhed the
entertainments of the day. Towards the
evening, all the company went down to
take the air on the Echelle, a fort of jttee,
that advances into the fea, to facilitate the
approach of boats.

The moon was juft appearing, and the
calmnefs of the evening invited us to go
on the water ; when the confufed cries of
men giving and receiving blows, apprized
us of the approach of the Boftandgy Bachi.
Nothing could be more alert than the women

men in hiding themfelves. The Drogman's Lady, and Madame de Tott, who
had nothing to fear, were alone able to
face this great officer, who made his appearance in an armed boat, with four and
twenty rowers. He had been juft chafti-
zing fome drunken fellows, and feizing
fome women rather too frolickfome, who
had fallen into his hands. He continued
his voyage, paffing along the pier, where
we faluted each other.

The pride of the runaway Greeks was
feeking an excufe for their fears, when a
fifherman paffing by, being afked what
route the Boftandgy Bachi had taken, fpread
a far greater alarm, by informing us, that
after having landed without noife at the
kiofk of a Greek lady, and liftened a few
minutes to the converfation, he had mounted into the window, with feveral of his
people, and that was all he knew of the
matter. But this was enough to make the
fright become general, as well as a fympa-
thy for the fate of the poor lady of the
kiofk; and they were all taken up with
thefe reflections, when the future hufband
of the younger daughter of the houfe arrived, once more to put her to flight, and

to

to fatisfy the eager curiofity of the company. "Make yourfelves eafy," fays he, to one of our female guefts, "your coufin and her friend have efcaped, with the lofs of all their diamonds, all their trinkets, and all the money they had about them : there was no time to hefitate ; the Boftandgy Bachi furprized, and feized them, to carry them off in his boat to prifon ; his avarice, however, brought him at length to reafon ; but he has left them much lefs contented with their evening than they had expected."

At this recital, the rage of the Greek women could no longer be reftrained ; and the difcuffions on the right, and on the fact, continued until they were interrupted by the noife of fome other fmall boats, which the fears of the Boftandgy Bachi magnified to an enormous fize. As foon, however, as all was quiet on his account, the converfation ran entirely on different fchemes for avoiding his perfecutions, and nothing elfe was talked of, until we faw him return down the middle of the Canal, towards Conftantinople. Every body was defirous of availing themfelves of the liberty he now had of taking the air, and in a

short

fhort time the fea was covered with a pro-
digious number of fmall boats, in which
the ladies were rowed to the found of mufic. Our company foon made part of the
little fleet. We coafted along the houfes,
and criticifed the proprietors, who from their
kiofks remarked on us in their turn; and I
gathered fome hints as we paffed along which
the Boftandgy Bachi might have turned to
good account.

I had, in preference, got into a fmall
boat with the future hufband, whofe coun-
tenance and gaiety interefted me. The
young man foon perceived that I was pleafed with him, and told me, in confidence,
his uneafinefs at not being able to fee his
intended bride. I felt for his fituation,
and promifed at a certain hour the next
day, to procure him a fight of her. He was
as punctual to the rendezvous as I had been
to furnifh him with the means of it; but
an unlucky flave, who watched him, was
very near difconcerting all my projects, by
giving the cry of alarm. The young lady
at the fame time perceived him, and was
making her efcape on one fide of the gallery, where I ran to ftop her at the entrance, calling my young Greek, who foon
came

came up to me. A reinforcement of two old harpies, however, ran from the bottom of the gallery, fcreaming like the geefe of the Capitol, but they could not arrive time enough to prevent a kifs of the future hufband, by which I was very happy to *Frenchify* the young folks ; we then delivered our prey into the poffeffion of the enemy. The father and mother approved of my little pleafantry, and the betrothed couple obtained the fame day the free fight of each other.

The Diako, a fort of ecclefiaftical preceptor, who was entrufted, agreeable to the cuftom in all Greek families, with the young lady's education, was the only perfon who blamed my conduct ; he fpoke of it with fuch warmth, as to make me conclude that he regretted the not being able to put a finifhing hand to the education of his pupil.

We remained fome days longer with the Drogman in the fame round of amufement of dulnefs or impatience. I returned home at length, to repofe myfelf, and there found Manoly Serdar, who informed me that another Greek, attached as he was to Racovitza, had juft abandoned him, to

enter

enter into the fervice of the Prince newly
nominated by the Porte. Manoly feemed
to me to exaggerate this crime with an af-
fectation which bore a very fufpicious appearance.

I endeavoured to perfuade him, that as
he might himfelf poffibly be liable, from
neceffity, to take a fimilar ftep, he ought,
from prudential motives, to ufe gentler
terms, and not to judge fo harfhly of a
man whom, perhaps, he was on the point
of imitating. " Look on me," fays he,
" as the worft of men, if ever I change;
and continue to efteem me, if I am not
guilty of fo black a treachery."   I pro-
mifed him one and the other; and I was
not long without being forced to keep my
word with him; he went off, in fact, a
few days after, for the purpofe, as he faid,
of trying fome further expedient in favour
of his benefactor; but I foon learnt that
he too had forfaken him, and attached
himfelf to the new Vayvode *. He wrote
to acquaint me with the ftep he had taken,
and to afk very humbly what I thought of

* This is the title beftowed by the Turks on the
Princes of Wallachia and Moldavia; they ufe alfo the
title of Bey.

G 5   him.

him. I was aware that circumstances might have rendered him excuseable, had he not himself aggravated his fault, by his protestations of honour and fidelity. I answered, therefore, that he had himself dictated the opinion I ought to entertain of his conduct, and that I should continue to preserve it with more firmness than he had maintained his principles.

This man rose himself to be Prince of Wallachia, during the last war of the Turks; but that situation has only afforded more scope to his intrigues, without any real display of talents, and I lost sight of him in that obscurity into which those ephemeral beings naturally return, who shine for a moment by the light of the despot, who gratifies at once his avarice and their pride, by selling them a transient glimmering of his authority.

We shall see Sultan Ofman obliged to employ that of an inferior officer in a matter relatively of little importance, but so singular as to be worthy of remark.

A drunken Janissary, pursued by the guard, who carry no other weapons in general than large sticks, availed himself of

the

the fuperiority he derived from his yatacan *
to defend himfelf like a lion; he had already difabled feveral of his enemies. an'
tigued with his own efforts, was
himfelf on the fteps of a khan †, to acquire
new ftrength, whilft the guard had changed
the attack into a blockade. The Grand
Signior, who frequently went through the
town in a difguife which deceived nobody,
happening to be at hand, approaches the
culprit, calls him by his name, orders him
to deliver up his weapon, and furrender to
the guard; but nothing moves the hero,
who, fupinely ftretched out, ftares at his fovereign, and menaces the firft who fhall
dare approach him. Sultan Ofman afks
him to what Orta ‡ he belongs. On his anfwer he fends for his Caracoulouctchi §. On

* A fort of large knife, very long and crooked at
the edge, which ferves inftead of a fabre.

† A public place, where merchants and travellers
are lodged.

‡ Company of Janiffaries who have no other name
than the number of the rank they have amongft each
other ; and in which the number of foldiers is unlimited. They reckon near thirty thoufand Janiffaries in the thirty-fifth company.

§ The cook of the company, who is alfo a ftaff
officer.

his

his arrival, " difarm that man," fays the Grand Signior to him, " and convey him to the Caſtle †."

The officer then loofened his girdle *, and holding it in his right-hand, he advances to the rebel, to whom he ſtretches out his left, faying, " Comrade, give me your knife, and follow me :" which was executed without reply, and with an air of the moſt perfect fubmiſſion. Prejudice will always have more empire over men than fear, more power than defpotiſm.

Sultan Ofman was very foon obliged to pay a tribute to that opinion to which he fell a victim. In vain the art of the phyſicians laboured to reſtore this Prince's health, whilſt the lofs of it was concealed, from political motives. He was obliged at length, however, finking under the diforder, to ſhut himſelf up within his palace, and re-

* The Caſtle of Europe, on the Canal, where thofe Janiſſaries are fent who are ordered to be ſtrangled ; and if they efcape from thence, they have at leaſt experienced the terror of it.

† A girdle of copper, that weighs 15 pounds, with which their officers can knock down a Janiſſary. The foldiers refpect infinitely this mark of rank, which, although fubordinate, is of great authority.

ferve

ferve his little remaining ftrength to enable him to attend the Mofque every Friday. This public ceremony, fanctified by
cuftom, cannot be neglected without excit-
ing the clamours of the military, and the
people.

The contradiction which appears on the
contemplation of a law that binds the defpot, vanifhes on reflecting that it is neceffarily dictated by the defpotifm of the multitude, the object of the defpot's perpetual
apprehenfions. Shut up in the impenetra-
bility of his Seraglio, the fight of him alone
can legally prove his exiftence. Without
this precaution, a Vifir formidable or artful
enough to command, or corrupt two or
three perfons after the death of his mafter,
might conceal it long enough to undertake
any thing with impunity.

It was not, therefore, without occafion-
ing very loud murmurs, that Sultan Ofman
omitted appearing one Friday in public; in
fo much, that to appeafe them, he determined to go the Friday following in ceremony
to Saint Sophia, the neareft Mofque to the
Seraglio, notwithftanding the ftate of debi-
lity and extreme langour to which his ill-
nefs had reduced him. On his return, already

ready tottering on his horfe, and fupported by the footmen who furrounded him, this Prince loft all fenfe between the two gates of the Seraglio. They threw a fhawl * over his head, and he died a few minutes after he was carried to his apartments.

The Vifir, the Mufti, and the great officers of the empire, repaired immediately to the Seraglio to verify the death of Sultan Ofman, and to compliment Muftapha the Third, the eldeft of Sultan Achmet's fons. The cannon of the Seraglio announced the fame day his death to the people, and the Muezzins †, together with the public cryers, proclaimed the new Emperor.

* A ftuff made of fine wool manufactured in Perfia and India, with which the Turks cover their heads, to guard them againft the cold, or to conceal themfelves. They have cloaks alfo to protect them ; but the Oriental Princes, when they appear in public, cannot avail themfelves of that protection from the intemperance of the air ; from cuftom they are obliged to go without it : the motives which induce them to appear, operate equally from covering themfelves with any thing which may prevent their being known.

† Muezzins, cryers of the Mofques who call the true believers to prayer, by repeating in a fort of finging tone, " God is great ;—God is God ;—There is only one God ;—Fly to Good works ;—Fly to prayers ; —God is God, and Mahomet is his Prophet." This laft phrafe contains alfo their confeffion of faith.

Mourn-

Mourning, in ufe amongft the Tartars, is not known to the Turks; but if that manner of honouring one's relations be indifferent to them, the precipitation with which they bury their dead, is certainly not a matter of indifference. It feems as if this nation, naturally fo grave and liftlefs, poffeffed activity only in this particular. Scarcely do they wait five or fix hours to perform this laft office to their relations, and the fear of burying a man in a lethargy, does not deter them *. Befides this abominable alacrity, the Turks who carry the bier, march with an extraordinary quicknefs, for the Mahometans believe that the foul fuffers until the end of the ceremony.

That of the Grand Signior's funeral differs from others only in the importance of the great officers who attend it to the Mofque. It is cuftomary for each Emperor to build one, and in the court of the Mofque

* The mifchiefs refulting from this ufage fcarcely ever come to light. I have, however, feen a Turk dug up, who had ftrength enough, in recovering from his lethargy, to cry out under-ground fo loud as to be heard; but he had ftill very nearly fallen a facrifice to forms, or rather to the fears which the Judge and the Iniàn, who had already received their fees, were under in reftoring him.

is

is the cupola, under which his body is to be depofited. In other refpects the Turkifh Emperors are buried as haftily as their subjects.

More than thirty years, which were elapfed fince the death of Sultan Achmet, father of the new Emperor, had not furnifhed him with very extenfive information. Confined during this long interval to his apartments, with fome eunuchs to attend, and fome women to amufe him, the conformity of his age with thofe Princes who were to be his predeceffors, left him little hope of fucceeding to the throne. But he had greater caufe of uneafinefs; his two brothers had given no heirs to the empire, at which the people had murmured during the laft reign, and frefh apprehenfions, or frefh murmurs of this kind, might coft him his life. Attempts had formerly been made on it, by the means which the barbarous policy of that country makes ufe of without fcruple towards the Princes who are near the throne: his own fufpicions, and knowledge of medicine, had preferved him.

This Prince, as well as his brothers, had very fhort legs, and appeared tall only on horfeback.

horfeback. A palenefs, attributed to the
effects of poifon, large eyes ftarting out of
his head, his nofe rather flattened, feemed
to indicate neither vivacity nor underftanding. The love of novelty, however, decided the multitude in his favour. The great
men thought him weak, and were in hopes
of governing him; the people hoped he
would be lavifh, and they were all miftaken. We fhall hereafter fee this Emper-
or in circumftances which will make him
known; and the kindnefs with which he
has diftinguifhed me, will give me the opportunity of developing the different fhades
of his character.

The firft care of an Ottoman Prince, after coming to the Throne, is to let his
beard grow *. Sultan Muftapha went a
ftep farther, and painted it black, that it
might be the more ftriking on the day of
his firft public appearance to have his fabre
girt on. This is the form of taking poffeffion; the Coronation of the Turkifh Emperor. This ceremony is always performed

---

* The Princes fhut up in the Seraglio, wear only
whifkers, as well as the young men, who only let their
beard grow to follow fome profeffion. They commonly call this becoming wife.

in

in the Mofque of Youb, a fmall village celebrated alfo for its earthen ware and dai-
ries, and which forms a fort of fuburb to
the city, towards the bottom of the harbour. Every thing was prepared for this
folemnity, and on the morning of the ninth
day, all the ftreets from the Seraglio to
Youb were lined on each fide by Janiffaries
in their drefs, and cap of ceremony, but
without arms, and their hands croffed on
their girdles †.

The minifters, the great officers, the
men of the law, and, in general, all thofe
perfons, who, from their fituations, are
attached to the government, arrive early at
the Seraglio, to be in readinefs to precede
the Grand Signior in the proceffion. This
march begins like our proceffions, by the
perfons of the leaft importance, who file off
without order. They are all on horfeback,
and each of them is furrounded by a group
of footmen, numerous in proportion to the
rank and fortune of the mafter. The men

† Except their red flippers and ftockings, large
blue breeches, and the bonnet, they are obliged to
wear, the Janiffaries drefs themfelves as they pleafe,
and the uniform is only diftinguifhable from the cut
of the cloaths.

cf

of the law are remarkable for the great fize
of their turbans and the fimplicity of their
horfes houfing; but the Janiffary Aga's retinue affords the moft fplendid picture in
the whole clafs of great officers. Befides
the number of fervants around his horfe, he
is preceded by two rows of Tchorbadgis †,
who march on foot to the right and left
before their General. Thefe principal officers, with yellow boots, the corners of their
robes tucked up within their girdle, each of
them carrying a white ftaff in his hand,
and his head covered with a helmet em-
broidered with gold, on the top of which
is a large plume of feathers in the manner
of the Romans, form a long alley of feathers, at the bottom of which is feen the
Janiffary Aga, who overtops the crowd of
his attendants; but an object of real curiofity is the habit of the Achetchy Bachi ‡,
who walks on foot between the two ranks
of Colonels, of whom I have been fpeaking,

† Colonel of the Janiffaries; the word literally is
' giver of foup."
‡ Head of the kitchen; each company has one,
who does the duty of Major; he fuperintends the living and the principal police. That of the Janiffary
Aga does the duty of Major General.

and

and only a few paces before this General. An enormous church veſtment of black lea-ther, ſtudded with ſilver nails, covers a bod-dice alſo of leather as ridiculouſly orna-mented.   This little waiſtcoat is fixed on him by a large girdle, with hooks and hin-ges, from which hang two enormous knives, the handles of which almoſt entirely cover the face of the Major ; whilſt ſpoons, cups, and other ſilver utenſils, ſuſpended by chains of the ſame metal, ſcarcely leave him the uſe of his feet. In faɛt, he is ſo loaded, that on all public occaſions when he is obliged to appear in this dreſs, two Janiſſaries attend him to bear up his garment.

The Tchaouche Bachi, one of the Miniſ-ters of the Porte, whoſe employment is eſ-ſentially connected with the civil admini-ſtration, is preceded by the ſergeants of whom he is the chief, and each of whom wears an oſtrich feather on the ſide of his turban.   The Boſtandgy Bachi is alſo pre-ceded by two files of Boſtandgis, ſtaff in hand, whoſe habits and head-dreſſes of ſcarlet cloth, preſent to the eye an unifor-mity far from diſagreeable. Theſe different officers of the empire ſalute the Janiſſaries to the right and left, who line the ſtreet, and who

who anfwer by an inclination of the body;
but they pay that homage with much more
refpeɛt to the turbans alone of the Grand
Signior, which are borne in ceremony before his Highnefs. Two of thefe head-
dreffes, with their tufts of feathers, were at
firft intended only as a change for the Emperor, in cafe he fhould think proper; but
that cuftom of pure convenience has become in the end an objeɛt of pomp and
oftentation.

Thefe turbans, placed on forts of tripods,
of filver gilt, are borne by two horfemen,
in their right hands, furrounded by a great
number of Tchoadars, and thefe officers
have only to incline the turbans a little to
the right and left, as the Janiffaries, to the
number of feven or eight at a time, bend·
moft profoundly to falute the Imperial
Aigrets.

In this proceffion, as curious to behold
as difficult to defcribe, the Vifir and the
Mufti, both clad in white, the former in
fattin, the latter in cloth, march by the fide
of each other, furrounded by their attendants, and preceded by two led horfes and
the

the chatirs * of the Vifir. On the fide of this Minifter, march the Alaytchaouches, †, who keep conftantly moving their filver ftaves, ornamented with fmall chains, not unlike childrens rattles, and the noife of which accompanies him even to his own Palace. A loaded waggon, clumfily made, badly carved, but richly gilt, contains a fmall fopha, and ufually follows the Mufti to receive him when he is fatigued.

At laft come the captains of the guards of the interior of the Seraglio, and the prin-cipal and inferior equerries, who precede the led horfes of the Grand Signior. Thefe horfes are covered with very rich houfing, which drag upon the ground, and leave nothing vifible but their heads, and their .fronts are ornamented with a tuft of herons feathers ; each of them carries alfo a horfe's tail, fufpended to the collar, and on the faddle a fabre and a pile of arms, paffed through the furcingle, are covered by a fhield. Each horfe is led by two footmen, who hold a long ftrap faftened to their

* A fort of footmen, diftinguifhed by girdles of filver gilt.

† A fort of tipftaff, attached to the dignity of Pacha.

heads ;

heads; immediately after follow two ranks
of Aſſekis *, with their ſabres ſlung acroſs
the body, and white ſtaves in their hands.
A troop of Zuluftchis ‡, with helmets of
ſilver gilt, and uplifted lances, march alſo
in two files, and precede the Peiſks. Theſe
latter in the Roman dreſs, carry the faſces
on the top of which is a ſilver axe, and
march before the ſolacks §, who, wearing a
ſort of buſkin, and armed with bows and
arrows, are adorned with a rich helmet,
crowned with a plume of feathers in the
form of a fan, which, joining at the extre-
mities, form two rows, in the middle of
which the Grand Signior marches alone on
horſeback. The Prince's tuft overtops this
magnificent group. His approach inſpires
a gloomy ſilence. The Janiſſaries make a
profound reverence until the row of feathers

* The Aſſekis are a picked corps from the Boſtandgis.
‡ The Zuluftchis are another ſort of troops for the
interior of the Seraglio; they are richly clad, and
wear two long curls of hair, which, faſtened to their
bonnet near the temples, came down as low as their
ſhoulders.
§ Solacks: This word means left-handed. They
are to defend the perſon of the ſovereign. They who
are on his right hand muſt draw their bows with their
left. This is, no doubt, the origin of their name.

hides

hides the Emperor from their view.   On
his fide, his Highnefs has the civility to anfwer this falute, by a flight motion of the
head, as he paffes, to right and left.

An infinite number of Tchoadars encom-
pafs and follow the Grand Signior.   They
furround alfo the Selictar Aga, who bears
the Imperial fabre on his fhoulder, and
wears a drefs of gold ftuff, which is the
only one amongft them that fits the
fhape.

The Kiflar Aga appears next, followed
by the Kafnadar Aga *, who clofes the
proceffion, and diftributes money to the
croud who follows him.   The Capidgilar
Kiayaffy §, and the Boftandgy Bachi, who
go before the Grand Signior on all public
occafions, on their return to the Seraglio
muft alight at the end of the firft court, to
be ready to precede his Highnefs.   They
quicken their pace accordingly; when they

---

* Every body knows that the Kiflar Aga is the
chief of the eunuchs; next to him is the Kafnadar
Aga, as black, and not lefs an eunuch than himfelf;
whofe employment is to take care of the private treafure, and to throw money amongft the people on
public ceremonies.

§ Captain of the Guards of the Porte.

come

come near, proftrate themfelves at his
horfe's feet, and introduce the Prince into
the fecond court, marching before him to
the place where he difmounts, and where
he is received by the domeftic officers of the
Seraglio.

The celebrated Rachub Pacha, who had
juft buried his old mafter, and inftalled his
new one, was the firft to perceive that Sultan Muftapha, to the full as ignorant, but
not fo inactive as he imagined him, muft
have employment. I have already painted
the character of this firft Minifter. It will
not, therefore, appear extraordinary that his
earlieft occupation was inhumanly to urge
his mafter to renew the fumptuary laws,
and to fee them carried into execution himfelf with the utmoft rigour. He was no
lefs defirous of encouraging his ignorance,
and of rendering his authority odious to the
public.

The firft acts of his authority were marked with violence and extreme barbarity.
The public cryers had not yet finifhed the
proclamation of the law, when the Grand
Signior difguifed, as well as the executioners of his pleafure who attended him, in-

Vol. I.   H   flicted

flicted punishments on such Greeks, Armenians, and Jews, as he found wearing the colours which are prohibited these three nations. An unfortunate Christian beggar, with an old pair of yellow * Morocco slippers, bestowed on him in charity by a Turk, was stopt by the Grand Signior, and this excuse was not sufficient to save his life. Every day gave birth to some new horror.

The Turks themselves were comprized in this law, which determined even the sort of furs permitted to be worn by each profession, and regulated the make of the cloaths, and the heighth of the head-dress of the women. The Europeans were only exempted, by submitting to wear their cloaths after their own fashion. This law alone, by subjecting them to it, ought for ever to have preserved the Ambassadors from the humiliation of seeing the persons they protected, bastinadoed and otherwise ill-treated, which the Turks would not have attempted if they had never given them any other than foreign dresses.

Two unfortunate events, however, made them relax in this profecution : it is only

* This colour is referved for the slippers of the Turks.

from

from fresh disasters that human nature, suf-
fering under despotism, is relieved from
those she already undergoes; and I shall
strengthen this remark by observing, that
when any person is asked his age at Constantinople, he always replies by quoting
the year of the great plague, of the famine,
the period of such a rebellion, or of such a
conflagration.

The Grand Signior's fleet was in the Archipelago, employed in exacting a tribute
from its wretched inhabitants, which they
always pay fourfold from this mode of collection; and the caravan of pilgrims for
Mecca, was on the road to Damascus.
Constantinople received at the same time
the intelligence that the Admiral's ship,
whilst the officers and greatest part of the
crew were on shore, had been run away
with, and carried to Malta by the slaves on
board; and that the caravan, in spite of the
Pacha, the cannon, and the troops that es-
corted it, had been attacked and cut to
pieces by the Arabs of the Desert. The
prejudices and vanity of the people, wounded at once by these two catastrophes, they
lost all respect, and the consternation encouraging their insolence, they had the har-

diness

dinefs to murmur loudly againft the Grand
Signior, and to impute to him thefe melancholy events.

Every thing which threatened the eftablifhed order with too hazardous a commo-
tion, muft neceffarily difturb Rachub Pacha,
and that artful Minifter foon difcovered an
expedient to divert the attention of the people, and point it to an agreeable object.
The famine ftill frefh in their minds, furnifhed him with the means. He circulated
amongft the public the magnificent project
of dividing Afia Minor by a navigable canal *, fit for the conveyance of provifions,
that the capital might no longer be expofed
to the rifk and uncertainty of fea voyages.
It would be neceffary for this end to join the
river Zachary to the town of Ifnic, the ancient Niceum, by means of a lake fituated
mid-way, the waters of which, by the conftruction of locks, and fupplied by feveral
rivers that might be turned into it, would
become inexhauftible. The Drogman of
the Porte was fent on a commiffion to M.
de Vergennes to demand my affiftance. I

* Rachub Pacha, better informed than the Turks
generally are, had borrowed this project, no doubt,
from Pliny.

went

went in confequence to the Porte to confult on a plan of operations, and even fome of the Minifters took journeys to gather information on the fpot ; but this whole project, which was only a pretext, vanifhed with the difcontents it had contributed to remove.

This event gave me the firft infight into the ignorance of the Turks, which I have fince completely verified. I was hardly arrived at the Porte before they prefented a Greek to me, who, as they faid, would be of the greateft fervice to us in the undertaking. He was the clevereft fellow in the empire : I afked him fome queftions on levelling, and was very foon able to appreciate his talents, on his fhewing me a fmall plate of copper with which he was to work, and which had at firft efcaped my notice, for this rare inftrument was furrounded by a great number of fpectators, ravifhed with admiration.

As for the unhappy pilgrims of the caravan, the matter terminated by looking on them as martyrs ; and his moft Chriftian Majefty having had the goodnefs to purchafe at Malta, and to reftore the veffel

and

and the Admiral's flag * which the flaves had carried off, calm was re-eftablifhed for fome time in Conftantinople.

The Grand Signior, however, fortunately found other employment for his activity than the fumptuary laws. The coin, the verification of the treafury accounts, very foon occupied his whole time. He retrenched alfo feveral abufes in the expenditure of his harem, and fixed the annual fum for the maintenance of his women †. The Kiflar Aga too, loft, under this reign, all the importance of his office in the adminiftration of the Vakoufs, which was given to the Vifir; but a fpeculation, always dangerous for the Sovereign, propofed to his Highnefs

---

* This flag was the more interefting, as having been given to the Grand Signior by Mecca, the Turks affixed a fuperftitious value on it. The names of the Prophet's Difciples at the four angles, a two edged fabre for the efcutcheons, and fome paffages of the Alcoran woven in filk, on a crimfon ftuff, for border, give this flag a talifmanic air, which always makes its lofs more painful than its poffeffion is of utility.

† I have been affured that the article of each woman's drefs was rated at two hundred and fifty livres a year, about ten guineas Englifh, which could not have been very fumptuous.

by

by one of his favourites, produced such a
diminution in the coin, that the false coin-
ers in Turkey work at this day in favour
of the people; no matter what alloy they
employ, the Grand Signior's coin is invariably below the nominal value of their
money.

The revenues of the empire were not
augmented by this manœuvre. The Pachas, who were at once the farmers of the
revenue, and governors of the provinces,
were not become less rapacious. The eye
of the Sovereign was only more attentively
fixed on their conduct, for the purpose of
despoiling them of the produce of their rapine * : their oppressions continued, and
the

* This species of confiscation is paid into the private treasury of the Grand Signior. The complaints
of the provinces against their governors, make him
acquainted with the fortunes of the oppressors; and
the Sovereign's justice highly offerded, no doubt, in-
demnifies itself, by taking possession of the sums extorted. The unfortunate wretches who cry distress,
obtain nothing but the culprit's head, and the new
oppressor who succeeds him, makes them almost always regret the former. The system of the Turkish
finances consists in placing on the surface a great
number of spunges, which swelling with the dew,
afford

the danger of appearing rich, did no more than check that prodigality which makes a fort of reftitution to the public.

Commerce, attacked in its circulation, very foon experienced that fort of langour which invariably produces the greateft diforders. The artizans were deftitute of work, and the want of employment, joined to need, hurried the people on to crimes. The hope of pillage, and the defire of revenging themfelves on the rich, multiplied the fires.

A *coundak*, a fort of combuftible that confifts only in putting a piece of tinder, wrapped in brimftone matches, in the midft of a fmall bundle of pine fhavings, is the method ufually employed by thefe incendiaries. They lay this match by ftealth behind a door which they find open, or on a window, and after fetting it on fire, they make their efcape. This is fufficient very often to produce the moft terrible ravages in a town, where the houfes built of wood, and painted with afpic oil, afford the eafieft

afford the Sovereign the means of acquiring all, by fqueezing them into a refervoir, of which he only keeps the key.

oppor-

opportunity to the firft mifcreant who is difpofed to reduce them to afhes.

This method employed by the incendia-ries, and which often efcapes the vigilance of the mafters of houfes, added to the com-mon caufes of fires, gave, for fome time, very frequent alarms ; but this fpecies of mifchief was at length put an end to, by the pregnancy of one of the women of the Seraglio ; and, above all, by the frefh acti-vity which this intelligence gave to com-merce. The prefents ufual on thefe occa-fions were prepared ; every thought was turned towards the *Donanemas* *, which had not taken place in the courfe of two reigns ; and the employment of individu-als, reftored the calm, the continuance of which this event infured, by adding to the weight of the Grand Signior's authority. In fact, of whatfoever fex the child in embryo might prove, this pregnancy at leaft pro-mifed heirs to the empire. Sultan Muf-

---

* The public rejoicings for the birth of the Otto-man princes. In general, when a princefs is born, they are given only on the fea, but it was determined that there fhould be extraordinary entertainments on the birth of the firft child of either fex, after fo long a fterility.

H 5 tapha,

tapha, more brilliant than ufual, appeared in public with a certainty of pleafing. Some money diftributed amongft the people, accomplifhed his popularity, which is always to be purchafed by condefcending to fpend a little money, and by fkilfully ufing a little addrefs to obtain it.

Murad Mollach had committed errors in this particular : he had not paid fufficient attention to the multitude. His friends apprized him, that in his fituation it was neceffary to ftand better with the people, if he wifhed to attain the firft employments. To pleafe them, therefore, and to ingratiate himfelf with his mafter, the Effendi, availing himfelf of the occafion, he prepared an entertainment for the event, which excited the public joy in the meadow of Buyukdéré.

I fhall not be blamed for dwelling on thefe details, which offer the genuine picture of the manners and cuftoms of a nation.

A rope was ftretched from the top of two pofts, placed at the diftance of forty feet from each other ; fufpended to this rope were feveral pieces of cord, with glafs lamps placed at proper diftances for the objects

jects the illuminations were intended to reprefent *. The Grand Signior's cypher,
the plan of his boat, a felection of words
from the Coran, applicable to the fubject,
ornamented the illumination during the
three days that the entertainment lafted,
whilft rope-dancers, a company of Jewifh.
players, and women-dancers, continued to
amufe the fpectators very late in the night.
But this picture appeared to me the moft
curious by the light of about twenty iron
chafing-difhes, raifed on ftakes, where a
conftant red flame was kept, by means of
pitched rags and fir-wood.

Thefe doleful chandeliers were placed
in a circle, to light the buffoons, who occupied the centre, and the tents prepared
for Murad Mollach and his company,
formed, with the croud of affiftants, a great
line of circumvallation, part of which was
occupied by the women of the populace.

* The principal Mofques are illuminated in the
fame manner during the Ramazan : their Minarets
ferve as pofts to faften the principal rope, from whence
the lamps are fufpended by rings, which flide along
as they are lighted from the gallery of one of the Minarets, and as from the gallery of the oppofite Mina-
ret they draw a fmall rope, that joins and fupports them
at proper diftances.

The

The illumination placed without this laſt
ring, ſerved only as the ſign of invitation
to the entertainment, the moſt precious
article of which was undoubtedly the Co-
medy.

A ſort of cage, three feet ſquare, and ſix
feet high, incloſed by a curtain, repreſents
a houſe, in which is one of the Jewiſh
actors in women's dreſs; another Jew,
dreſſed as a young Turk, and ſuppoſed to
be in love with the lady of the houſe; a
valet, no bad buffoon; another Jew in woman's cloaths, playing the lady of eaſy
virtue; a huſband who is duped; all the
perſonages, in ſhort, one ſees on every
ſtage, occupied the exterior, and compo-
ſed the piece. But what one ſees no where
elſe, is the *denouément*; every thing paſſes
on the ſtage, nothing is left to the imagination of the ſpectators; and if the cry of
the Muezzin † happens to be heard during
theſe tranſactions, the Muſſulmen turn towards Mecca, whilſt the actors continue
their parts. And I ſhall have ſaid enough
of this whimſical aſſemblage of momentary

* The perſon who at the top of the Miranets calls
the people to prayer.

devo-

devotion, and continual indecency, if the reader perceives that this picture, difficult to defcribe in writing, would be ftill more fo for the pencil.

A fet of aukward rope-dancers, and clnmfy wreftlers, fome vulgar buffoons, and ftrolling women dancers, filled up the interval between the Comedies. Amongft thefe women, whofe merit certainly does not confift either in the elegance of their fteps, or in the gracefulnefs of their atti-tudes, but who give infinite pleafure to the Turks by fuch talents as they poffefs, one young girl of ten or twelve years old, of ve-ry promifing agility, was particularly diftin-guifhed; and after each dance, when fhe went round, as was the cuftom, with the Diare *, to collect in money the value of thofe agreeable ideas with which fhe had furnifhed the company, the principal Turks of Murad Mollach's company put her up to auction, bidding one againft another, placing fequins at the fame time on her forehead †, as a mark of their favour. The value

* Tambour de bafque, that ferves to mark the meafure.
† The Sequin is a gold coin fo light, that by placing it on the forehead it fticks fometimes, and this is the manner

value of this slave, whose face, notwith-
standing, had nothing extraordinary to
distinguish it, rose to the sum of twelve
purses *, which an old Mollach gave the
merchants, as the price of the barren plea-
sure of perpetuating those ideas which he
had lost the hopes of realizing.

Except at the public entertainments,
where the licence is unbounded, and permitted, the actors never display their talents, but in private houses, where they are
sent for on feasts or weddings. These
companies of wretched mountebanks are
always composed either solely of men or
women. The companies of women repre-
sent the inside of the Harems with as much
distinction, and as little reserve, as the co-
medians of whom we have been speaking;

manner in which the Turks reward the agility of the
dancers.

* The purse is of the numerical value of 500 piaftres, and which would be equal to 1500 livres French,
or 62l. 10s. sterling, if the adulteration of the Grand
Signior's coin was not carried so far, as no longer to
admit of comparison, and which the Exchange of
Commerce has since reduced to 25 or 30 per cent.
but without reaching the level of the comparative value of the intrinsic specie.

but

but mufic is the common and moft familiar amufement of the Turks.

Their martial mufic is of the moft bar- barous kind ; enormous drums, ftruck with a kind of mallet, mix a dead noife with the clear and lively found of the fmall kettle- drums, which are accompanied by clarinets, and the fhrill trumpets, the tones of which they force to complete the moft difcordant crafh that can be imagined.

Their chamber mufic, on the contrary, is very foft ; and if one is difpleafed with the monotony of femi-tones, which at firft is very difagreeable, one cannot but allow it a fort of melancholy expreffion, with which the Turks are very powerfully af- fected. A violin with three ftrings, tuned to the Jew's harp, the viol d'amour, which they have adopted, the Dervife flute, fofter than our German flute, the tambour, a fort of mandoline, with a long handle, and wire ftrings, the reed, or Pan's flute, and the tambour de bafque, to mark the time, ufually compofe their orcheftra. It is pla- ced at the bottom of an apartment, where the muficians, fquat upon the ground, play melodious, or quick airs, without written mufic, but always in unifon, whilft the

company

company in profound filence, get intoxi-
cated with an enthufiaftic langour, by
fmoaking their pipes, and taking pills of
opium.

Thofe amongft the Turks who give
themfelves up to an immoderate ufe of opium, are eafily to be diftinguifhed by a fort
of ricketty complaint, which this poifon
produces in courfe of time. Deftined to
live agreeably only when in a fort of drunkennefs, thefe men prefent, above all, a
curious fpectacle, when they are affembled
in a part of Conftantinople, called *Teriaky
Tcharchiffy*, the Market of Opium-eaters.

It is there, that towards the evening, one
fees the lovers of opium arrive by the different ftreets which terminate at the *Soly-
mania* *, whofe pale and melancholy coun-
tenances would infpire only compaffion, did
not their ftretched necks, their heads twifted to the right or left, their back bones
crooked, one fhoulder up to their ears, and
a number of other whimfical attitudes
which are the confequences of the diforder,
prefent the moft ludicrous and moft laugh-
able picture.

---

* The greateft Mofque in Conftantinople.

A long

A long row of little fhops is built againft one of the walls of the place where the Mofque ftands; thefe fhops are fhaded by an harbour, which communicates from one to the other, and under which every merchant takes care to place a fmall fopha for his cuftomers to fit on, without hindering the paffage, who place themfelves in fucceffion to receive a dofe proportioned to the degree of habit and want they have contracted The pills are foon diftributed; the moft experienced fwallow four of thefe, larger than olives, and every one drinking a large glafs of cold water upon it, waits in fome particular attitude for an agreeable reverie, which, at the end of three quarters of an hour, or an hour at moft, never fails to animate thefe machines, and make them gefticulate in a hundred different manners; but they are always very extraordinary and very gay. This is the moment when the fcene becomes moft interefting; all the actors are happy; each of them returns home in a ftate of total ebriety, but in the full and perfect poffeffion of a happinefs which reafon is not able to procure him. Deaf to

the

the hootings of the paffengers they meet with, who divert themfelves by making them talk nonfenfe, every one of them firmly believes himfelf in poffeffion of what he wifhes; they have the appearance and the feeling of it: the reality frequently does not produce fo much pleafure.

The fame thing happens in private houfes, where the mafter fets the example of this ftrange debauch. The men of the law, the moft fubject to it, and all the Dervifes, ufed to get drunk with opium, before they learnt to prefer the excefs of wine. There are in Turkey two kinds of this fpecies of Monks, very different from each other, but equally remarkable. The diff.rence between them proceeds from the fort of regulation that their founder has impofed refpectively upon them; that of the Mewliach Dervife is to turn round like a totum, to the found of a tolerably foft mufic, and to acquire a holy intoxication from the vertigos, which are the natural confequence of this ftrange exercife, if habit did not prevent that effect, which, however, they generally make up for at the tavern. The cuftom of the other Monks, called

called *Tatta-tepen* *, is more doleful, and more favage. It confifts in gravely marching one after another round their chapel, and pronouncing the name of God with a loud voice, which they ftrain at every ftroke of a drum beaten on the occafion ; but very foon the ftrokes gradually following clofer, become fo loud, that thefe wretches are obliged to make great exer· tions of their lungs, and the moft devout never finifh the proceffion without fpitting blood. The appearance of thefe Monks is always gloomy and auftere, and they are fo perfuaded of the fanctity of their practice, and fo fure of pleafing Heaven by their howlings, that they never look on other men but with the moft profound contempt.

There are other Monks alfo in Turkey, and Santons, who go about the country : it is dangerous to meet them in a wood ; under the cloak of religion they get admittance to the houfes of devotees, and are every where the worft company one can find.

* Beater on boards. Perhaps in the beginning they had no other inftrument.

Such

Such of the Dervifes as are impudent
enough to profit by the general ignorance,
fet themfelves up for prophets, and pro-
phecy unpunifhed.   If the event has jufti-
fied the predictions they have hazarded,
they pafs immediately for faints, and are
held in the higheft eftimation ; but even
thofe who are unfuccefsful pafs only for
fools, but do not forfeit their right of admittance every where.   Nothing can refift
their effrontery ; the name of God, proftituted by thefe knaves, has always an influence on the fuperftitious multitude ; and
I have feen one of them come and feat
himfelf with the greateft infolence, by the
fide of the Vifir, whilft I was in fecret converfation with him, and people of the higheft rank were kept at a diftance.   The fanaticifm of the public compels a tacit fubmiffion in the more enlightened, and the
moft powerful Turks cannot get rid of this
rabble for a moment without giving them
money, the only effect of which is to render them more troublefome and infolent.

Rachub Pacha, better informed than the
Turks are in general, whether with a view
of deftroying ignorance, or to leave behind
him a monument of his tafte for literature,
                                                built

built at his own expence, a large dome, for the purpofe of founding a public libra- ry, there being no fuch inftitution at Con- ftantinople. A thoufand or twelve hun- dred Arabic or Perfian manufcripts, which the Vifir had collected and bequeathed to this library, were ranged on fhelves, dif- pofed in the form of circular pyramids, in the centre of the rotunda. A librarian was appointed, the public had the right of en- tering at ftated hours, and Rachub found- ed the neceffary expence. But nothing certainly will ever lay the foundation of the inftruction of the Turks, as long as the difficulties of their language prefcribe its limits to the fole talent of reading and writing.

The prefs might have extended them : one Ibrahim Effendi had eftablifhed that ufeful art of multiplying copies ; he even printed feveral works, but which had a very indifferent fale, although he felected the moft promifing. But what fuccefs, in fact, could be expected from an art, which on the firft glance, reduced to nothing the talents of thofe who paffed for men of knowledge ? They became at once judges and parties in their own caufe : the art of
printing

printing could not attain the perfection of joining the letters; it was defpifed, and Ibrahim fhut up fhop.

Rachub himfelf was not free from that falfe fcience which takes a pride in over-coming difficulties. He amufed himfelf with joining the letters fo as they could not be decyphered; and above every thing, he delighted in playing upon words: many ftrokes of this bad kind of wit, tolerably pleafant, are ftill recounted of him, but which, from the very circumftance of their belonging to the Turkifh gloffary, cannot be tranflated.

Difengaged by the natural energy of his mind from all thofe prejudices which de-grade almoft univerfally the Turkifh na-tion, this Vifir derived a fource of enter-tainment even from the moft atrocious ob-jects. We may fuppofe that Mahometan-ifm itfelf did not efcape his pleafantry.

An European prefents himfelf one day at the Porte, and fignified by his geftures more than by his language, that he wifhed to become a Turk, and that he was a Ger-man. Befides the neceffity of calling fome perfon who could underftand him, it is exprefsly ftipulated by treaties, that no

European

European can lawfully renounce his religion but in the prefence of a Drogman.—
One of the interpreters of the German em-
baffy was found, and conducted to the Vifir,
whom he informed that the new comer was
a native of Dantzick, which place he had
quitted exprefsly for the purpofe of embrac-
ing the Mahometan religion at Conftantinople. This refolution appeared to Rachub
too fingular not to excite his curiofity to
know the real motive ; and the candidate,
queftioned a fecond time, devoutly replied,
—" That Mahomet had appeared to him
in a vifion, to invite him to merit all the favours beftowed upon his followers."——
" There is a ftrange rogue for you !" fays
the Vifir, " Mahomet has appeared to him
at Dantzick !—To an infidel ! when, notwithftanding the exactnefs with which I
have faid the five prayers to him for more
than feventy years, he has never done me
that honour. Tell him, Drogman, that
nobody deceives me with impunity ; that
he muft, doubtlefs, have killed his father
and mother ; that I will order him to be
hanged up, if he does not tell me the
truth." Terrified at this menace, the traveller confeffed that he had been a fchool-
master

mafter at Dantzick, and that after fome
time, he had been fo unlucky as to furnifh matter for fome difagreeable fufpicions: that the parents of the boys entrufted
to his care had cruelly perplexed him ;
that, at length the magiftrates were difpofed to handle him a little roughly ; that
to efcape from their fentence, and well informed that at Conftantinople they did
not make fuch a ftir about fuch a trifle, he
was come to change his head-drefs, in
hopes of being very foon himfelf fufficiently inftructed to contribute alfo to the education of the Turkifh youth. " Make
him declare his confeffion of faith," replied the Vifir, " and take this convert to
fuch a Mollach's houfe, who muft provide
for his fupport : they are formed for each
others fociety ; I make him a prefent of
this comrade ; but let the Iman of the
quarter be told to go and inftruct them
both, and acquaint them, *that no religion
has ever tolerated their doctrine.*

The practice regularly purfued by the
Turkifh Emperors of building and endow-
ing a Mofque, has fo multiplied thefe temples, that building-ground was become
very fcarce at Conftantinople.   Sultan
Maha-

Mahamout had determined to erect one at Scutary; he died, and Sultan Ofman finifh-ed it. Muftapha, however, found means to purchafe in his capital a piece of ground large enough for the Mofque which he in-tended building. This Prince, to fupply the deficiency of thofe houfes he was about to deftroy, and to endow this new Mofque, had formed the project of making a jettée, on a fhallow bank of the Sea of Marmora, near the walls of the city, there to form a new quarter.

The ignorance of the architects ftrove a long time, and under great difadvantages, againft the waves of the fea; and avarice, which learns to its coft, that there is no true œconomy but in well placed expences, was at length compelled to give way to ne-ceffity; all the money which had been la-vifhed until that time was thrown away; every thing muft be begun at frefh ex-pence; caïffoors were employed, and this expedient fucceeding, the work was com-pleted.

The principal part of the Turkifh pro-prietors of houfes, purchafed for the fite of the Mofque, became inhabitants of the new buildings, and renters of the new temple,

Vol. I.   I   which

which was finished under the reign of its founder. The interest or religious zeal of the proprietors presented no obstacle to Mustapha in the purchase of such houses as were convenient for his plan. Sultan Soliman, the greatest Ottoman Prince, was not so fortunate in similar circumstances; and the anecdote in question appears to me the more interesting, as it may give some idea of the legal value of property in Turkey.

The site of the projected Solimania was fixed on, and Sultan Soliman seemed to have no impediment to fear in the necessary purchases; when a Jew, possessor of a house of little value, refused to part with it at any price. The most tempting offers were made him without success. The Israelite remained inflexible, and his obstinacy prevailed over his avarice. Every person of Sultan Soliman's Court, accustomed to see the universe bend before this Prince, anticipated with applause the prospect of seeing the Jew's house razed from its foundation, and the Jew himself dragged to condign punishment; but fortunate are those Princes who do not confound the man with the Sovereign, nor imagine they have a right to exercise their authority to gratify

their

their perfonal refentment! Fortunate the
Princes who ftay till juftice pronounces in
their caufe, and whofe minds are fo enlar-
ged as to look beyond the applaufes of their
furrounding courtiers!

Such was Sultan Soliman.—He defcended from the throne to interrogate the law.
" A man," wrote he to the Mufti, " in-
tends raifing a temple to the divinity; all
the Muffulmen, proprietors of the ground
neceffary for the purpofe, haften to partake
of the good work, by felling their houfes;
one perfon only, and he a Jew, obftinately
refufes every offer:—What punifhment
does he deferve?"—" None," replies the
Mufti; " the property of individuals is
facred without diftinction, and a temple
cannot be erected to God whofe very foundation refts on the violation of fo holy a
law.   It is favourable in this inftance to the
Jews apparent defire of leaving his children
a property, the value of which might otherwife be diffipated; but this ground may be
rented, that is the Sovereign's right whenever he has occafion for a houfe. An agreement muft, therefore, be made with the
Jew and his heirs for a certain annual rent;
by this means his property will remain in-

I 2   violate,

violate, the houfe may be knocked down, and the Mofque built without fearing that the prayers of the Muffulmen will be rejected." The Mufti's fetfa was carried into execution.

It is ufual on founding Mofques, to add the endowment of public fchools, where the children of the diftrict go to learn their prayers. Many rich perfons build fountains alfo, and Namas-Giack * to point out to devout Muffulmen the direction of Mecca. This fort of luxury difplays itfelf with profufion, particularly in the country. Superftition has multiplied thefe little eftablifhments; they are worth a great number of indulgencies, and the Turk who obtains them has a daily demand.

Thofe, of which perfons in office are in continual want to fave themfelves in this world, are purchafed rather higher; and the neceffity they are under of preferving the Grand Signior's favour, furnifhes a temptation for avarice, ambition, and fear, to make innumerable fpeculations, and very

---

* Ground laid out for prayers. A ftone on which the profeffion of faith is ufually written, points out the direction of Mecca; whilft a fountain ferves the Muffulmen for ablution.

often

often erroneous calculations. The moſt œconomical method, undoubtedly, when it ſucceeds, is to obtain the Grand Signior's acceptance of a ſlave that pleaſes him, and who will be grateful enough to uſe her intereſt in favour of her former maſter. I have ſeen, at my mother in law's, one of thoſe Georgian women deſtined by Sultana Aſma to the ſuperlative honour of amuſing his Highneſs, and I perceived nothing very ſtriking in her more than a girl of eighteen years old, of a middle ſize, very robuſt, and who might paſs for a good pretty alehouſe wench. She had, it muſt be owned, large black eyes, the beauty of which, common enough in Turkey, would have diſtinguiſhed her in any other country; but they were inanimate, and the *ſurmé* they were blackened with did not render them more agreeable.

I will not incur the reproach of neglecting to ſpeak of the drug ſo celebrated, and ſo much made uſe of throughout Aſia. It is a black, impalpable powder, ſo volative that it adheres in a ſort of dew to a braſs wire, fixed to the cork of the flaſk which contains it. The art of uſing it conſiſts in drawing out the braſs wire, of which the

cork

cork forms the handle, without touching the edges of the flask, so as to shake off the black powder. They put the point of this needle into the inner corner of the eye, keeping the eye-lids open at the same time, and draw it gently acrofs towards the temples, fo as to leave two black ftripes within the eye-lafhes, which give a very harfh air to the handfomeft eyes; but which the Turks take for an air of foftnefs.

But what will appear ftill more extraordinary, is, that the men themfelves, and, above all, the old men are guilty of this coquetry. The ufe of *furmé* is almoft general. It is fuppofed, 'tis true, to poffefs the virtue of ftrengthening the fight; but it is more certain that the effect of *furmé* is difagreeable to that fenfe †. Every thing which

---

† This practice is lefs common amongft the people, and feems to be more particularly confined to the ftate of opulence, and a fort of inaction neceffary to this kind of beauty; for it is evident that this impalpable powder, laid ever fo carefully on the edge of the eyelids, would fpread itfelf difagreeably by a copious perfpiration. That clafs of the people, however, always moft numerous, whofe labour exacts a daily tribute from idle luxury, has likewife its peculiar mode of decoration, which confifts, as in almoft all favage nations,

which can contribute to the prefervation
of beauty, or fupply the want of it, is
fought after in this country with extreme
eagernefs, and the *Chiotes* * at Conftantinople are in poffeffion of this quackery.
But never has their art of rendering the
fkin frefh, protracted the moment when it
naturally ceafes to be fo. They may be
accufed with more apparent juftice of ac-
celerating the deftruction of beauty in
Turkey, did not the immoderate ufe of hot
baths ruin it more effectually than the
fulimé †.

nations, in covering the arms and legs, and fometimes
the breafts, with figures pricked out on the fkin, and
which being rubbed, before they are healed up, with
fome colour, preferve that which penetrates. The
blue produced by gun-powder is the moft in ufe; and
their prejudices furnifh the principal fubject of thefe
fantaftical defigns. The names of Jefus and of Mahomet, diftinguifh the Chriftian and the Turk employed
at the fame labour. Gallantry has likewife its fhare
in this fort of ornament, and one very often fees amo-
rous verfes intermixed with paffages from the Alcoran;
but this fpecies of gallantry is not always fufficiently
determinate to prevent errors on the fubject.

* Inhabitants of Chios.

† Sulime is a fort of paint to whiten the fkin and
make it fhine.

The

The conftruction of thefe baths ought to be defcribed, that after examining their effects, we may be able to eftimate the confequences. Two fmall chambers of brick, lined with marble or ftucco, communicate with each other, and are refpectively lighted by fmall domes, perforated in the form of chequers. This fmall building is joined to the houfe by an apartment to undrefs in. Double-lafhed doors, lined with felt, fhut in the firft and fecond part of the bath. A fubterraneous vault, to which one enters from without, ferves to heat it. This vault is of the fize of the lower apartment, and heats alfo a cauldron placed directly under the marble floor of the bath, up to the very cieling of the vault below, where a fire of dry wood is kept. Funnels placed in the middle of the walls, run from the infide of the cauldron, and rife without the cupola, to carry off the evaporated water, which is kept conftantly boiling. Other pipes, concealed alfo in the mafonry, run from a refervoir, and convey cold water into the building, by means of cocks placed at the fide of thofe which convey the hot water. Little alcoves of well polifhed wood are difpofed in the form

of

of feats, and gutters cut out of the marble carry off the water.

Thefe private baths, always heated four and twenty hours before-hand, are by thefe contrivances carried to fuch a degree of heat, that after ftripping quite naked in the outer chamber, and putting on very high wooden fandels, to prevent the feet being burnt on the marble floor, one cannot ftill advance into the firft apartment without giving the lungs time to dilate between the two firft doors, and this dome ; it is impof-fible to proceed into the fecond bath, under which is the real ftove, without taking the fame precaution ; and it may fafely be pro-nounced, that the air of this apartment is to that of the firft, as that is to the exter·nal air. A fudden perfpiration, which ftreams from every pore, is the firft effect on entering, but the violence of that heat, and of its effects, do not prevent the women from remaining in thefe baths five or fix hours at a time, and from ufing them very frequently.

They who have not private baths, fre-quent the public ones, which are always prepared to contain a great number of peo-ple.

I 5   Some

Some women, however, more delicate and fcrupulous than others, take the baths for themfelves, whither they are accompanied by their female friends, and where, to complete the entertainment, they take their dinner. The charm of a greater freedom, and that of converfing together all the day, are deemed a fufficient recompence, no doubt, for the difagreeable choice of their place of rendezvous.

. The women bathers, called *telleks*, with little bags of ferge in their hands, rub the fkin till it is dry. They make ufe alfo of a very fine clay, kneaded with rofe leaves, and afterwards dried in the fun, to rub the head with, as a fubftitute for foap, pouring hot water on it at the fame time from large metal cups. The womens hair thus cleaned and perfumed, is then plaited in a number of little treffes.

The reader will not find, in this defcription, the pearls, the diamonds, the rich ftuffs, and all the charms with which Lady Mary Montague has fet off thefe baths. One can fcarcely believe, either, that her Ladyfhip really entered them with all her cloaths on, as the publifher of her letters

has

has made her fay *. It is very certain,
however, that a too frequent ufe of thefe
baths opens the pores at length to fuch a
degree, as to render them fenfible to the
eye; and it is no lefs certain, that fo violent a dilatation of the fibres, by impairing
the fhape, brings on decrepitude before old
age.

Thefe public baths, difperfed in great
numbers through every quarter of the
town, ferve alfo for the men; but not at
the fame hours fet apart for the women. A
man who fhould dare attempt to enter when
the women are affembled there, would be
feverely punifhed for his rafhnefs, even
fhould he have the good fortune to efcape

* In the new edition of that Lady's letters, we are
affured that every thing contained in them has been
verified. This affertion of the editor ought, in my
opinion, to be accompanied with proofs and autho-
rities. But the public is never difficult on the fubject
of errors which amufe them. Intereft, which profits
by this facility, is not more fcrupulous; and they who
only love the truth, muft limit themfelves to a faith-
ful expofition, without undertaking to defend it.

the

the taffes *, the fandals †, and the wet pef-
temals † that would be thrown at him. The
Turkifh women are implacable when the
only object of the men is to infult them;
but one cannot, without horror, caft an eye
on the fatal confequences of that exceffive
debauchery to which they fometimes aban-
don themfelves. I do not fpeak of thofe
women whofe beauty is fo often proftituted
for money, and whofe mutilated corpfes I
have feen in the environs of Conftantinople. The atrocious barbarity of thofe men
who affaffinate them to fave their money, or
to avoid the danger of being apprehended
in bringing them back to the city, can only
be explained from motives of avarice or fear.
I fpeak of women of a higher condition,
who are hurried away by an ungovernable
paffion, and efcape clandeftinely from their
prifons. Thefe unfortunate women always

---

* Taffe, a Turkifh word, in Englifh, cup, the pro-
nounciation and meaning of which is French.

† Sandal; this word has alfo the fame connection
with the French language; it is a wooden fole that fits
the foot, and is faftened by a thong; but there is this
difference in Turkey, that their fandals are raifed on
two crofs pieces of wood, five or fix inches high.

‡ Peftemal, a piece of ftuff made of filk or cotton,
which is referved for modefty in the baths.

carry

carry off their jewels, and think they can
poſſeſs nothing too precious for the man
who receives them.   The fatal inclination
which leads them aſtray, prevents them from
perceiving, that it is to theſe very riches they
owe their ruin.

The villains whom they go in ſearch of,
ſeldom fail to puniſh their inconſiderate raſh-
neſs after a few days poſſeſſion, and to make
ſure of their effects by the moſt monſtrous
of all crimes ; but which this government
is the leaſt vigilant to puniſh.   One often
ſees the naked bodies of theſe unfortunate
wretches floating in the harbour, under the
windows of their murderers ; yet theſe tre-
mendous examples, ſo well calculated to in-
timidate the women and to calm this furor,
neither frighten nor correct them.

It is to prevent the more frequent repetition of theſe diſorders, during the ſolemn
feaſts and public rejoicings, that the government totally prohibits the appearance of women.

The pregnancy announced in the Seraglio, was now near its term of expiration ;
all the preparations for the entertainments
were completed, and nothing was wanting
but

but the order of the government to begin them.

It is only fince my intimacy with the Turks, that I have learnt with any degree of certainty what paffes on occafion of births in the Seraglio, and I fhall give the detail in this place, to avoid recurring to the fubject.

On the firft pains of labour, the Vifir, the Mufti, the great officers, and heads of the military, are fent for to the Seraglio, to wait the moment of the delivery, in the Hall of the Sopha, for fo they call the inter-mediate apartment * which feparates that part of the Seraglio called the harem, from the reft of the buildings occupied by the Grand Signior and his houfhold.

Twelve pieces of cannon, four pounders, and which are called the cannon of the. fo-pha, are ranged along this chamber, which looks upon the fea. There is alfo a battery of Swedifh cannon, fituated in the Cyprefs Wood, which is very improperly called the garden of the Seraglio, half way between that and the walls of Byzantium, which

* This room in private houfes is called Mabin Odaffi, the literal meaning of which is, the intermedi-ate chamber.

form

form the inclofure of the Palace, and which are lined without with a monftrous artillery, whofe fire croffes that of the battery of Tophana fituated on the other fide of the harbour.

As foon as the Sultana was delivered, the Kiflar Aga came out of the Seraglio with the child, which was a Princefs; he prefented it to the grand officers, who prepared the regifter of its birth and fex, after which the pieces of the fopha gave their falute, which being heard only by the battery half way, was repeated from thence, and followed by thofe from the point of the Seraglio, and from Tophana. To thefe different falutes, fucceeded thofe from the Cuftom-houfe, from the Admiralty, and from Leander's Tower *. The public cryers immediately publifhed

---

* This tower, fituated on a detached rock, facing Conftantinople, and nearer Scutary than the capital, is called, by the Turks, Kis-Couleffy, the Girl's Tower. They pretend that it ferved long as a prifon for a Greek princefs.—The name the Europeans give it, makes one prefume that it was formerly looked upon as the dwelling of Hero, but we muft be always very circumfpect in this fort of conjectures, to avoid ridicule, and even abfurdity. Some travellers have placed a pillar of Pompey at the mouth of the Black Sea, where
that

publifhed this event, and the new-born
Sultana was proclaimed *Eibe-Doullach*, giv-
en by God.   Public rejoicings were ordered
to continue feven days on the land, and
three on the water, which was never practifed heretofore, but on the birth of a
Prince ; but it was thought neceffary to do
that honour to the firft born after two barren reigns.   Thefe entertainments anfwered
the purpofe alfo of gaiety, of which there
was much need ; and though they were very expenfive, and a heavy burthen to the
people, even the merchants confoled themfelves for the neceffity of fhutting up their

that illuftrious Roman never was ; they have called
another pillar one fees at Alexandria by the fame
name, which certainly was never raifed by Pompey.
And to return to the environs of Conftantinople :—
There is an old tower on the borders of the Euxine
Sea, which remains amongft the ruins of feveral others
of the fame conftruction, built in a line at equal diftances, which ferved in former times to give the alarm
by fignals on the appearance of Coffack veffels, whofe
piracies were very formidable to the inhabitants living
on the Black Sea.   This detached tower, in this re-
gion of romance and barbarifm, was without a name,
and we Europeans, who have the rage of wifhing to
know and explain every thing, called it after the tower
celebrated by Ovid.

fhops

shops in seeing despotism equally suspend its operations.

In fact, all the instruments of tyranny, who in general serve only to oppress humanity, appear to have no other occupation than to patronize licentiousness in these times of public rejoicings. On these occasions, the Saturnalia of ancient Rome are revived at Constantinople. The slaves have liberty to breathe, to make merry before their masters, and even to be merry at their expence. New actors take possession of the stage, the great are presented with a picture of their own foibles, and, confounded with the people, are obliged, from custom, to laugh at it themselves, or at least to assume that appearance.

As for the rest, one may easily conceive that a government, which from its very nature seems to smother every sentiment of joy, cannot compel it to appear, without retiring itself out of sight, and that poor human nature, always easily imposed on, always ready to adopt every flattering illusion, no sooner loses sight of her tyrants, than she eagerly avails herself of a moment's relaxation to snatch a feeble and transient glimmering of happiness.

The

The Greeks, above all, naturally gay and riotous, give themfelves up, on thefe occafions, to all the intemperance of joy, making a quick tranfition from oppreffion to happinefs, from humility to infolence.

Let us here take a view of the fcenery of this new theatre, and place the actors on the ftage. Pofts, fixed at three or four feet diftance, before the fhops, and on the edges of the foot-way, on each fide of the ftreet, are joined together at the top by arches, which extend alfo to the houfes. This flight wooden roof, covered with branches of laurel, mixed with curled paper of different colours, forms the bowers, to which are fufpended tinfel leaves, which the leaft wind puts in motion with a ruftling noife, whilft their glittering furface reflects the light of the glafs lamps, and coloured lanthorns, with which the whole building is decorated. The gates of the houfes of individuals are likewife ornamented with an elegance proportioned to the importance and vanity of the proprietor ; but the houfes of the great exhibit the higheft excefs of magnificence in their decorations. The ftreets adjoining are covered to a certain diftance in the form of bowers, of a fufficient

cient heighth to prevent the lamps and tinfel work from ftraightening the paffage for
perfons on horfeback; and thefe porticos,
thus decorated, are continued even into the
inner courts of their palaces, where halls,
built exprefsly for the occafion, richly furnifhed and lighted by a quantity of luftres,
whofe light is reflected from an infinite
number of glaffes, offer to the curious a
place of repofe, in which the mafter of the
houfe does the honours according to the
quality of his guefts. Others content themfelves with furnifhing the lower part of their
gateway, and the two folding doors thrown
open, invite the paffenger to ftop and take
a difh of coffee or other refrefhments ordered by the mafter, and with which his fervants are always eager to fupply.

The gate of the Vifir, and that of the Janiffary Aga *, are above all remarkable for

* Pacha Capouffi and Aga Capouffi, the gate of
the Pacha and the gate of the Aga, fignify the houfe
of the Vifir, and that of the General of the Janiffaries.
One of the common people, or even a perfon inferior
to him of whom he fpeaks, fays, alfo I have been, or
have ferved at the gate of fuch a one ; but the term
Capou, or Capi, Gate, pronounced fingly, always means
the Prime Minifter's Palace, the place where all great
affairs are difcuffed.

the

the fumptuoufnefs of their decorations, and the profufion of trinkets which are whimfically interfperfed with the richeft ornaments. One cannot help beholding, with aftonifhment, the hall of the Divan, that dreadful tribunal, that terror of nature, dreffed out and difplayed, only for a few days, the image of gladnefs.

Twenty lanthorns, on which are painted ludicrous and often obfcene figures, mixed with tranfparencies, infcribed with the name of God, of his attributes, the Grand Signior's cypher, or fome play upon words. Pieces of looking-glafs cut into the form of funs, to give a brilliancy to the illuminations, amufe the multitude, whofe numbers never diminifh. Thofe perfons, who, from their age and the importance of their ftations are naturally the moft ferious *, are equally

* The defire of obliging one of my Turkifh friends had induced me to carry a toy which was rather pretty to his fon ; the child feemed very happy with me, and I entertained myfelf with the pleafure I was about to give him, when at the fight of the plaything, I perceived him fhorten his ftep, walk. gravely into the room, look at my prefent with a marked indifference, fit down in the moft ferious manner, and wrap himfelf up in his little haughtinefs. Soon after comes
in

equally delighted with thefe trivial and pue-
rile imitations. I have feen a little palace,
of glafs clipping and ifin-glafs, made by an
European, fold for three thoufand livres,
about one hundred and twenty guineas, to
the Vifir, to make a figure in his temporal
fhop.

So much profufion at the houfes of the
Minifters and of the great men, would lead
one naturally to imagine, that on fuch an
occafion the illumination of the Seraglio
would greatly furpafs all the others.

A ftring of lamps decorates the firft gate,
and fome coloured lanthorns light fuch paffengers as curiofity leads towards that which
feparates the two courts. This gate, as well
as the firft entrance, is very fcantily lighted; fufficiently, however, to enable one to
diftinguifh fome old colours, great hatchets
and fhields, fome piles of arms, and fifh

in the grandfather, and by a moft fingular contraft,
the old man launches out on the neatnefs of the workmanfhip, fits down on the carpet to admire it, turns
it over, examines it minutely, plays with it, and
finifhes by breaking it. This fcene at firft appeared
ftrange to me, but a more thorough knowledge of
Turkey, has fince taught me every thing in that country worthy of obfervation, either in point of fingularity or inftruction.

bones,

bones, which pafs for thofe of giants, and other objects of as great importance *. But the gate of the Armory, which is on the left on entering this court, prefents many very curious articles of ancient armory †. The Mint, more agreeably decorated, exhibits a very different picture. An infinite number of lamps, from a tapeftry of new piaftres ‡, ifolettes §, paras ||, and fequins ¶, are arranged in various forms. This is alfo the only place in the Seraglio where the curious

* In the firft rejoicing, an old bifhop's mitre, amongft other trophies, was fufpended to the keyftone of the roof.

† The moft remarkable article in this depofitory is a Catapulta, which is the only one exifting; but the Turks make fo little account of it, that it was only by chance in fearching the magazine, that I difcovered this precious morfel of antiquity, buried under a heap of rubbifh. This magazine of arms was formerly a Greek church.

‡ Money equal to half a crown.

§ About a fhilling and ten-pence halfpenny, or thirty paras.

|| A fmall piece of filver, of a farthing value.

¶ A piece of gold of more or lefs value, and the moft generally known called Zeremapouls, are at prefent worth feven fhillings and fixpence Englifh, allowing always for the difference of 20 per cent. on the Grand Signior's money, by the exchange with Europe.

are

are even tolerably received by the Zarpha-na Eminy ‡. If every thing in the city announces that defpotifm has left an open field for the greateft exceffes of a fanatic joy, the truly mournful afpect of the firft court of the Seraglio, makes us feel that the interior of thefe formidable walls is ftill that impenetrable afylum, where defpotifm, in a liftlefs anxiety, awaits the hour to put an end to the intoxication of a momentary liberty, which animates every individual.

In fact, this exceffive gaiety of the people can only be looked upon as a fit of phrenzy, which might alarm the defpot, if he permitted it to laft. I have already faid that the Greeks diftinguifh themfelves in a peculiar manner by their infolent and unbounded joy. The Jews, on the contrary, always occupied by commerce, always tormented by the thirft of gain, after profiting as much as poffible by the fabrication and fale of lanthorns, make a trade of their buffooneries before the houfes of the great, where *paras* are diftributed to every Merry-Andrew who prefents himfelf.

‡ Infpector of the Mint.

Many

Many perfons in office have ftationary
comedies before their houfes, on various
fubjects, but always of the moft indecent
kind, which are performed to the great fatisfaction of the public; and in thefe pieces
the government itfelf is as little refpected
as manners. One fees every moment companies of Greeks and Jews reprefenting the
different officers of the empire, and exercifing their refpective functions to turn them
into ridicule. In one of thefe entertainments, at which I was prefent, the drefs of
the Grand Signior himfelf, and of all his
retinue, were treated with the fame difre-
fpect. A company of Jews had the pre-
fumption to mimic him; it is true, that
this infolent imitation was foon put a ftop
to, but they ftill continued to counterfeit
the Grand Vifir, and, of courfe, no other
officer was fpared.

I faw, amongft others, a fictitious Stambol Effendiffy ‡ who was permitted very
quietly to exercife pretty fevere diftribu-
tive juftice. Chance threw him in the
way of the real one; they very gravely ex-
changed a falute, and proceeded on their

‡. Lieutenant of Police of Conftantinople.

way.

way. Another troop, who had counter-feited the Janiffary Aga, went and took poffeffion of this General's houfe, whilft he was taking his rounds, and his fervants treated the mafque with as much diftinction as if he had been their mafter. Thefe pleafantries were followed by other ftrokes of wit not quite fo agreeable, but which had the fame licence. Pretended directors of bridges and caufeways, followed by paviours, took up the ftones before the doors of feveral individuals, who were obliged to buy themfelves off at a confiderable price. Other mafques, in the drefs of fire-men, obtained ranfoms in a different manner. In a word, all forts of extortion were practifed; and to perfect the illufion, they were acted to the life. All this, however, became at length burthenfome and inconvenient; but the ftated time expired, the cudgel again appeared, and order was refumed †.

Vol. I.   K   Defpotifm

† The Befiftins prefent in the Donanemes the richeft coup-dœiul; that of the jewellers is particularly brilliant in precious ftones, which the merchants expofe there, and thefe covered markets are really moft curious and moft truly magnificent objects. The Tcharchis, other markets, where all forts of drugs are

Defpotifm was conftrained, notwithftanding, ftill to refpect liberty during the
three evenings deftined for the fire-works
on the fea.

The Marine corps, the corps of Dgebedgis ‡, and of the artillery, had each of
them prepared an entertainment of fire-
works for three fucceeding nights.

Some large rafts towed into the middle of
the harbour, oppofite to Yaly Kiofk §,
where the Grand Signior was to be, were
difpofed in fuch a manner, as to exhibit
the confolatory fpectacle of the taking of
Malta, or of fome engagement in which
the Mahometans infallibly get the better of
the Chriftians. A great number of pe-
tards, fo much fmoke, and fo little fire,
that in the cleareft intervals one could

are collected, appear to me alfo to be tolerably well
decorated.

‡ Dgebedgis ; there is no refemblance between this
and any of our corps. Their duty is to take care of
the arms, powder, and all fuch implements of war as
are kept in magazines.

§ The Kiofk of the Admiralty ; it is fituated without the Seraglio, on the fea fhore, and is made ufe of
for all the ceremonies relative to the fleet, as well as
for the embarkation and difembarkation of the Grand
Signior.

fcarcely

fcarcely diícover the walls of the pafte-
board caftle that was attacked, give no very
high idea of the talents of the fire-workers;
neither is their fuccefs very brilliant in the
art of firing íky-rockets. The greateft
part of thefe rockets, after havirg languifh-
ed on the fcaffolding, are extinguifhed in
the fea before the cafe has time to take
fire.

The gerb-rockets, lighter and better
proportioned, rife a little higher; but in
general they light very flowly, from the
aukward difpofition of their matches, and
go off in very irregular directions: it muft
be owned, however, that even thefe de-
fects give an air of profufion and duration
to the Turkifh flower-pots, which makes
them very pleafing. The general applaufe
does not take place until the moment when
unfortunate Greeks or Jews, hired to wear
European dreffes, and to defend the place
attacked with a few ferpents, which are
foon expended, are affaulted, overturned,
and on account of their drefs, are beaten
with the fift, according to the rights of war,
and which, in their character of infidels,
they are permitted to return.

K 2   The

The pleafure of knocking down and beating the Chriftians is fo high a regale for the Turks, that Sultan Mahamout's favourites, in other refpects very amiable, could contrive nothing better for their mafter's amufement, at an entertainment they gave him in the Seraglio, and the fubject appeared to them fo fimple, and fo natural, that they made no fcruple of requefting the European Ambaffadors to lend them their wardrobes. They put thefe cloaths on the backs of Jews, always deftined to be beaten, and always ready to take a beating when they are paid for it. All the Grand Signior's courtiers agreed that thofe fellows had never earned their money better than on that day.

The Jews might certainly do as they thought proper; but was it neceffary to lend thefe cloaths? and ought not our Europeans to have felt the difagreeable confequences which always follow from allowing themfelves to be thus turned into ridicule?

Thefe rejoicings were fcarcely finifhed, before a frefh pregnancy was announced, which produced Sultan Selim; and the Princefs Eibé-Doullach, the firft child,

was

was married at fix months old, to a Pacha eftablifhed in his government, whom it was more their intention to plunder than to favour, and who felt very forcibly the neceffity of making an annual remittance of one hundred thoufand piaftres, for the maintenance of his young wife, as well as for the honour of fo defirable an alliance.

Milek Pacha experienced alfo a difagreeable circumftance of the fame kind, which muft ftill more fenfibly have hurt him.—Young, amiable, and arrived at the office of Captain Pacha §, he enjoyed quietly within himfelf the pleafure of having only one wife, who occupied all his attention, and who loved him tenderly. The goodnefs of his mafter had juft raifed him to the dignity of Vifir ||, and nothing was wanting

§ A Captain Pacha; at fea this dignity is equivalent to that of Admiral; but it cannot be compared with it when the fleet is laid up. That place only gives the rank of Pacha with two tails. It is fometimes held, however, by Vifirs of the Bench; that is to fay, by fuch Pachas as, from their rank, wear the fame bonnet as the Grand Vifir, and have a feat at the Grand Signior's Divan during their ftay at Conftantinople.

|| All the Pachas of three tails are called Vifirs.—This dignity, therefore, muft not be confounded with that

wanting to complete his happinefs, when a
fifter of the Grand Signior, a widow for
the fixth time, faw him pafs at a public
ceremony. Struck with Melek's handfome face, the old Sultana demanded him
of her brother, who immediately fignified
to the Admiral that he intended honouring
him with his alliance. This came upon
him like a clap of thunder; but there was
no remedy, and Melek was obliged inftant-
ly to part with his wife, who furvived this
misfortune only a few days; but the Pacha, more refolute, or lefs fenfible, re-
figned himfelf to circumftances. He continued to pleafe; nay, he was even fuch a
favourite, as to induce the Grand Vifir to
rid himfelf of fo dangerous a rival, by obtaining for him a government, which freed
him alfo from the careffes of his antiquated
Princefs ‡.

Sultan

that of Grand Vifir. This laft is diftinguifhed by the
great feal of the empire; the Grand Signior's fignet.
He poffeffes the chief inftrument of defpotifm. On
this account he is called Vizir Azem, or the Grand
Vifir.

‡ We have already feen that the Sultanas cannot
go out of Conftantinople. Defpotifm fears, no doubt,
that in letting them remove to a diftance with their
hufbands

Sultan Muftapha continued to employ himfelf in his finances,. by affiduoufly ftripping the accomptants,. and by applying to his own ufe, in confifcations, what thefe knaves had been ftealing in the empire. Already did his Highnefs enjoy the fatisfaction of having completed feveral *baf-nés* ‡, and fealed them up ; but this was a very infignificant gratification of his ruling paffion ; he was determined to attempt the fortune of the Pacha of Bagdad. The independant conduct of that Governor, held out, in fact, more than one pretext for the defire of defpoiling him ; but it was much

bufbands the male infant which might be born would efcape the blow.

‡ Hafne fignifies treafure, and is made ufe of for the whole of the Sovereign's treafure. But it is alfo ufed as an expreffion of number, and in that cafe means 10,000 purfes, which, with the difference of exchange, is equal to about fifteen millions of French livres, or about 875,000l. fterling ; and the feal is put on the coffers when this fum is completed, as it is ufual in France to feal a bag containing 1200 livres. Muftapha took fuch pleafure in this occupation, that he facrificed every thing to increafe his treafure : he fold a great many of his trinkets by auction, and even fent to the Mint all the gold and filver veffels given him by the Court of Denmark on the conclufion of their treaty with the Porte.

easier

eafier to pronounce the order than to carry
it into execution. Wealth and diftance are
very efficacious weapons of defence.

Muftapha flattered himfelf that he fhould
be able to effect, by furprize, what he
could not hope to accomplifh by threats.
A Capidgi Bachi §, apparently the bearer
of a mark of friendfhip, but actually provided with an order, addreffed to the Judges
of the Divan of Bagdad, to ftrike off the
Pacha's head, waited on him. The Governor on his fide, attentive to all the
emiffaries of Conftantinople, and knowing
the fucceffors of the Greek empire well

§ Capidges Bachis, a fort of Chamberlains who
take under the arm every body who is admitted to
the Grand Signior's audience, and conduct them to
his Highnefs. They are likewife employed in all the
extraordinary commiffions which have for their object
the execution of the Sultan's orders of every kind. To
collect provifions, to raife troops, to confirm a Pacha, to extort money from him, to cut off his head,
or after they defpoil him of his wealth, to conduct
another into banifhment, very often to poifon him by
the way; all this is in the Capidgi Bachi's province;
thefe are perquifites of his office. The Salachors,
(ufhers) are employed in the fame duty in cafes of inferior refort, and their advancement depends on their
making ufe of more or lefs addrefs in the execution of
their orders.

enough

enough to fear them and their prefents *, made the Capidgi be fearched before he was introduced into the Divan ; and finding the fecret order, commanded the bearer's head to be cut off, and fent it as his only anfwer to the Grand Signior. Similar attempts were attended with the fame fuccefs, and thefe examples, imitated by other Pachas not fo rich nor fo remote as that of Bagdad, encouraged refiftance, and reduced the Porte to the laft refource, of affaffinating or poifoning fuch of its officers as it was difpofed to punifh. In this cafe the emiffary, difguifed as much as poffible, and furnifhed with an order which he keeps clofely hid, endeavours to approach the profcribed perfon ; choofes, if he can, the time of the affembling of the Divan, feizes the favourable moment of killing his man, prefents his order, and runs no further rifk if he is fkilful enough not to mifs his ftroke. This is what may be called fignal juftice ; but poifon requires lefs courage, and on that account begins to have the preference.

* Timeunt Danaos et dona ferentes.

K 5   Such

Such of the Pachas, or other oppreſſors, as by a cuſtomary retribution of a part of their rapine, know how to ſatiate the rapaciouſneſs of the ſublime Porte, enjoy the portion they reſerve in a ſort of ſecurity; but they can preſerve their fortunes after their death only by intruſting it to the perſon who manages their affairs, or to ſome friend on whoſe probity they think they can rely. Theſe confidential truſts, however, expoſe their poſſeſſors to very terrible dangers; and the fear of loſing their lives, or at leaſt their own fortunes, often tempts to infidelity. To theſe motives may perhaps be added, the ſo natural temptation of appropriating to themſelves the effects of the deceaſed, in a country where the words honour and honeſty are ſcarcely known.

One may form a correct judgment of the proceedings of the Turkiſh government reſpecting ſucceſſions, from the manner in which the Exchequer ſettled its accounts with the perſons employed by Rachub Pacha, who had long ſince married a ſiſter of the Grand Signior.

That Viſir, celebrated for his activity of mind, the atrociouſneſs of his character,

and

and the fubtlety of his fpirit, died in office, and in poffeffion of a degree of favour, which left no reafonable caufe of uneafi-nefs to thofe who tranfacted his affairs; but his fortune rendered them accountable, and the exaggerated calculations of Sultan Muf-tapha might prove them defaulters. The feal, however, was put in his Highnefs's name, who referved to himfelf the inquiry. into the fucceffion.

A Turk, who had filled the office of Treafurer to the late Grand Vifir, was ar-refted the inftant the feal was placed, as well as an Armenian, who had always been that Minifter's bank; thefe two unfortu-nate men, chained in the prifons of the Se-raglio, fuffered every moment the terror of that death with which it pleafed their keepers to infpire them. They were obliged to pay for their food its weight in gold; and the fmalleft accommodations, the moft trifling comforts were fold to them at the moft exorbitant prices. At length they gave in their accounts, and the examination which the Grand Signior took the pains to make himfelf, only ferv-ed to evince their innocence; but rapaci-oufnefs, deceived by this inquiry, had recourfe

courfe to tortures to obtain the avowal of a
fuppofed fecret truft which never had exifted.

The Boftandgy Bachi was charged with
this horrible perfecution ; the moft fcan-
dalous calumnies of informers were liftened
to ; enormous fums were fuppofed to have
paffed fecretly through their hands, and
the moft cruel torture was employed, in
vain, as to the difcovery of any thing, but
with great effect for the avarice of the
Prince, who fwallowed up the greateft part
of the riches which the Armenian derived
from his father's commerce. The Treafurer underwent the fame fate, and was
compelled to purchafe his life at the price
of his whole fortune, after having fuffered
the moft dreadful torments.

Such is the juftice exercifed by the defpot, *legally* no doubt, fince there is no law
to counteract thefe barbarities, and the
habit of fubmitting to them ftifles even
complaint.

Here let us examine the kind of juftice
adminiftered by the Turkifh tribunals, from
a written code, refpected by opinion, and
commented on by magiftrates appointed
for that purpofe. And you, who juftly

offended at the inconveniences and multi-
plicity of our judiciary forms, have ven-
tured to affert, certainly without reflection,
that Turkifh juftice was preferable to ours,
examine attentively the picture I am about
to offer to you; and if you are able, try
to point out fome remedy for that fuper-
fluity which is fo injurious to us; correct
our intemperance, but never make a boaft
to us of poverty.

The Grand Signior is at once the fucceffor to the Caliphate, and the chief of
the military government; his defpotifm is
founded on the Coran, and the expofition of
that book is exclufively allotted to the body
of Ulemats; every thing muft bend before
that law; every thing muft be obedient to
the Sovereign. Thefe two powers derive
from the fame fource, and one already perceives the clafhing and differences which
muft arife between two powers poffeffed of
equal right, but whofe interefts are at
war; one fees, alfo, that the power of mutually injuring each other muft frequently
unite, and compel them to reciprocal at-
tentions and compliance.

If the Ulemats, in fact, can interpret the
law at their pleafure, and animate the people

ple againſt the Sovereign, he can, with one word, depoſe the Mufti, ſend him into ex-ile, and even deſtroy him, as well as all thoſe of his body who may incur his diſpleaſure. The law and the deſpot ought equally to fear and reſpect each other; but the deſpot, if he be not an ideot, neceſſa-rily inclines the balance; he diſpoſes of all the treaſure, of all the employments, and of the lives of all his ſubjects. He has terrible means of enforcing obedience.

Now let us inquire into the uſe of power, whether on the part of the Grand Signior, or of the Judges.

The more extenſive the power of the Grand Signior, the more difficult is it to limit the power of thoſe officers who re-preſent him. The Pachas throughout the whole extent of the Ottoman empire, are the governors and the renters of their Pa-cholicks; they appoint ſub-governors and under-renters in every diſtrict; theſe again diſtribute other under-renters, to the full as tyrannical; ſo that in this cruel hierar-chy, each ſubaltern receives the double of the ſum for which he ſtands accountable.

If the renter can exerciſe his right over the annual revenue in ſo deſtructive a man-ner,

ner, the governor of each province, armed with a more extensive and more formidable power, demolishes with more unlicensed boldness and facility. It rests with him to multiply the persecutions, the extortions, and depredations, which are bounded only by his rapacious desires. The slightest pretext is sufficient to summon to his tribunal, such as he is pleased to call to account; and the rich, at the feet of the infatiable man, is never innocent.

The Sovereign, however, apparently a silent spectator of these transactions, delays the punishment of the oppressor only until the produce of the oppression be sufficient to merit a place in his private treasury; but although the Grand Signior seems only to watch the man in office, in vain would the rich man attempt to escape from despotism by concealing himself in obscurity; he is very soon invested with an employment, which, sooner or later, furnishes the Prince with the right of calling him to account. This man has no other resource, therefore, than by making others account to him in the same manner, and by converting the fruit of his rapine into ready money, the more easily to conceal it. We have

have already feen that the men of the law
are the only perfons who can enjoy their
fortune in tranquillity, and I fhall not fpeak
of the Chriftian fubjects, or the Jews.
Thefe, defpifed and infulted even by the
Muffulman porter who ferves them, are only refpected by the government becaufe their
induftry accumulates thofe riches of which
daily oppreffion produce a reflux through
the channel of men in place, into that gulph
where every thing is fwallowed up by the
Sovereign.

From the accounts of Europeans one may
be led to believe, that the Turkifh Cuftom-
houfe is not fo rigorous as that of other nations. The Franks, it is true, pay only
three per cent. I will not bring to account
the extortions they fuffer befides of every
kind; they are foreigners; their fituation
has no connection with the inquiry into the
manners and government of the native inhabitants. Thefe latter pay feven per cent.
Cuftom-houfe duty, and ten on many articles of confumption; by an affected cle-
mency alfo, of which they make a great
boaft, this duty is allowed to be paid in
kind; but what is the confequence? That
on a hundred turbots which a fifherman

brings

brings to market, they take ten of the fineſt, which alone are worth all the little fry they leave him.

Let us now conſult their books of law, and ſee how they contrive to interpret them in their tribunals.

Every judgment ought to be founded on the depoſition of witneſſes.   This is the firſt law of the Arabian legiſlator.   The plaintiff and the defendant, therefore, cannot appear in court without being provided alike with witneſſes; there is no trial therefore without falſe witneſſes.   The art of the Judge conſiſts in diſcovering, by inſidious interrogation, to which of the parties he ought to aſſign the preference of allegation; and this primary judgment decides the proceſs.   If one party denies, the other is intitled to prove ; ſo that, brought into a lawſuit by a man whom I have never ſeen, for the payment of a ſum I never owed, I ſhall be obliged to pay him on the teſtimony of two Turkiſh witneſſes who will ſwear to the debt.—What means of defence are left me ? Only to admit that I owed the money, or to inſiſt that I have paid it.   If the Cady be not already bought off, he will adjudge me witneſſes, whom I ſhall very ſoon find, and
it

it will coft me only a trifle for the perfons who will perjure themfelves for me, and the duty of ten per cent. to the Judge who will give me my caufe.

He who gains, always pays the expences; the apprehenfion, therefore, of lofing the money one has, does not check the defire of poffeffing onefelf of that of others; and the punifhment prefcribed for the fuborners of falfe witneffes, and for falfe witneffes themfelves *, muft feldom be inflicted : the Judge whofe revenue they increafe, owes them fome indulgence.

A Turk wanted to rob his neighbour of a field of which he was the legal poffeffor. This Turk begins by making himfelf fure of a fufficient number of witneffes ready to fwear that the field had been fold to him by the proprietor; he then applied to the Judge, and gave him 500 piafters to get him to authorize his ufurpation. This ftep, which proved fufficiently the iniquity of his demand, incenfed the Cady; he diffembled, however, heard both parties, and finding

* The punifhment of perjury is to lead them through the ftreets on an afs, with the culprit's head towards the tail of the animal; but I never faw that law carried into execution.

that

that the lawful poffeffor would oppofe only the ineffectual defence of his title of poffeffion ;—" You have no witneffes then ?" faid he to him ; " Well, well ! I have *five hundred* who depofe in your favour !" He then produced the bag, which was the intended price of his corruption, and fent off the corruptor.

This inftance, which does honour to the integrity of the Judge, does not undoubtedly do much honour to the law itfelf. That is always the fame, and every Cady does not refemble this.

In complicated caufes, befides witneffes, the parties have the precaution to obtain a fetfa of the Mufti ; but thefe, as I have already obferved, being given only by the head of the law from the ftate of the cafe laid before him, each party obtains a favourable one without any difficulty.

The affair, however, is not terminated by a formal judgment pronounced in your favour. The only certainty is the expences : if the adverfary ftarts a new incident, the procefs muft be renewed, and frefh expences incurred.

The right given by the Turkifh civil law to every individual of pleading his own caufe,

caufe, would be undoubtedly a moft inefti-
mable privilege; but what advantage can
he derive from it in a country where the
decifion is arbitrary? Hence it is that the
Jews, the Armenians, and the Greeks,
have preferved to their chiefs a fort of civil
jurifdiction, to which they fometimes fubmit, to prevent the object of the law fuit
from being confumed by the Cady who is
to judge it; but excepting the Jews, who
are more fuboidinate to their Kakam than
the Chriftians to their Patriarch, it is common enough for the party aggrieved to fum-
mon the other to the Turkifh Courts, which
finifh the matter by enriching themfelves
with the fpoils of both.

The law refpecting flaves, fubmits them
entirely to their purchafer, calls upon him
to treat them well, or to fell them if they
do not pleafe him; and their teftimony is
inadmiffible either for or againft their mafters.

A Greek, of the name of Draco, extremely rich, had two handfome country-houfes
near the village of Terapia, on the channel
of the Black Sea, at three leagues diftance
from Conftantinople, where he paffed the
fummer with his whole family, and feveral
Chriftian

Chriftian flaves who waited on him.   In his neighbourhood was a dock-yard : one of the Turkifh fhip-builders availed himfelf of the opportunity to intrigue with one of the Chriftian flaves.—Draco furprized, and ill-treated her; and to revenge herfelf, fhe fet fire to two houfes, which were totally confumed.   After this act of wickednefs, fhe had the daringnefs to boaft of it; and Draco, juftly dreading the further effects of this wicked wretch's fury, had her carried off by night, and conducted to a Jew's houfe, with orders to fhut her clofely up, and to fell her as foon as poffible, fo as that fhe never might return.   She found means, however, to cry out of the window that fhe was a Turk.   The populace affemble, the guard arrives, the Jew's houfe is forced open, and the girl is led before the Vifir; there fhe again declares herfelf to be a Turk, detained by Draco as a flave, and ill-treated by him to compel her to become a Chrifti-an; and that fhe had fet fire to his houfes to fave a female Muffulman.   Her zeal was highly extolled, thanks were returned to Providence, and Draco was hanged two days after the fire, before his own houfes, ftill fmoking from the conflagration.

It

It will be afked, no doubt, what was become of the law which refufes to admit the
teftimony of flaves againft their mafters,
that which condemns an incendiary to the
flames, and the other which allows the
accufed to plead his own caufe? Nothing
of all this was thought of : a Chriftian does
not merit fuch attention in Turkey.

After having feen the innocent perifh,
let us now fee in what manner the law treats
the guilty. It is not to be repeated without
horror; but it is for thefe monfters that the
law has fome refpect. The law which condemns a murderer to death, permits the
neareft relation of the deceafed to grant his
pardon. The criminal is conducted to the
place where the crime was committed; the
perfon who does the office of executioner,
performs alfo that of mediator! he negoci-
ates even to the laft moment with the neareft of kin to the deceafed, or with his wife,
who ufually follows, and affifts at the execution. Should the propofals be refufed,
the executioner does his duty ; if they are
accepted, he leads back the criminal to the
tribunal, to receive his difcharge. Thefe
compofitions, however, feldom take place,
from a fort of opprobrium attached to the
idea of felling the blood of one's relations,

or

or one's hufband; but we muft be fenfible that if fuch a law exifted amongft us, we fhould fometimes fee the moft cowardly and moft execrable affaffins enjoy in peace the fruit of their enormities.

A young Turk, anxious to inherit his property, had murdered his father, and was condemned, on the ftrongeft evidence, to lofe his head. One of his friends, a companion of his debaucheries, flies to the Judge with a confiderable fum of money; there he learns that the fentence is already pronounced: ftill he is not difcouraged; he preffes the Judge, already gained by the fight of the money:—" I cannot," faid he to his client, " acquit your friend, without a proof of his innocence ftronger than that on which he was convicted.—Have the courage to declare yourfelf the murderer of his father; produce two witneffes to prove it; I fhall condemn you to the fame punifhment which has been pronounced againft your friend; from that moment he will be reftored to all his rights, and it will reft with him to grant your pardon." The undertaking was undoubtedly hazardous: a parricide is not calculated to infpire much confidence. The criminal, however, pardoned the fuppofed posed murderer ; and this atrocious transaction, sanctified by the law, had the most complete success.

To punish even highway robbers, it is necessary to apprehend them in the fact. The legislator of the Arabs owed this indulgence, no doubt, to a nation which existed only by rapine. The Grand Signior's territories are infested therefore with those robbers, who are called *haidouts*, where they commit the greatest horrors ; and the few efforts made by the government to check them, and which are always made in the most aukward manner, only serves to disperse and drive them from the capital.

If they commit some murders in a village, the Cady, who repairs to the place, extorts a sum of money from the inhabitants, without taking the trouble of searching after the offenders. On this account the first care of the inhabitants is always to keep the crime from the knowledge of the Judges, whose presence is more formidable than that of the robbers.

The latter are in Turkey like unprivileged workmen in our towns. They are punished if caught at work ; they quit their trade on becoming rich, talk over their exploits,

ploits, and arrive at employments which give them the right of exercifing their induftry.

The tenet of the Coran enjoining fub-miffion to the decrees of Providence, does not appear very well adapted to a criminal code. A Turk, however, having killed a Chriftian, by a violent blow of a ftick on his fkull, the Judge, after making them produce the murderer's weapon, and well, and duly examined the quality of the wood of which it was made, pronounced that it was too light to have produced the Chrifti-an's death without the direct will of Provi-dence, which it did not become human be-ings to oppofe. It would not be very eafy to turn to that chapter of the Coran from whence this fentence was extracted; but it appears indubitable, that if the Chriftian had committed the murder in queftion on the Turk, the Judge would never have ima-gined that he was executing the decrees of God.

Befides the law-fuits which follow the ufual judicial forms of informations, verifi-cation of titles, and appeals to the fuperior courts, all private quarrels, and charges in the firft heat of paffion, immediately referred to the tribunal, on the requifition of one party, which the other muft not hefitate to accept, particularly if the quarrel has taken place before the people. At the fole word, juftice, one fees the multitude invariably taking a part againft him who avoids it : the name of juftice is ,facred in all nations. It is the central point of the human mind. One may form erroneous notions of it, one may labour to deceive others, and may even impofe upon onefelf refpecting it ; ftill juftice reigns imperceptibly, and vice, as well as virtue, is conftrained to do her homage.

Each quarter has its Mekkemé *, where a Cady, attended by his Naib †, fits every hour of the day, to hear complaints, and to diftribute juftice with the more expedition, as the expences are always paid after the fentence.

The juftice exercifed by the Stambol Effendiffy § refpecting every thing which concerns the fupply of the capital, appears more

* Mekkeme ; a tribunal of juftice.
† Naib ; the Judge's firft clerk.
§ Stambol Effendiffy, the Lieutenant of Police of Conftantinople ; it is the firft ftep by which the men of the law afpire to the great offices, which, as well as this, are all in the Grand Signior's nomination, without regard to feniority of rank.

difin-

difintereſted, but has only a more noble and more majeſtic appearance. He fixes the price of articles, cauſes it to be publiſhed, and examines into the integrity of the weights and meaſures, either perſonally, or by a deputy, called Murtaſib. Preceded by four Janiſſaries in their formalities, and with ſtaves in their hands, this officer goes through the city on horſeback, one of his people carrying by his ſide a pair of open ſcales; another carrying weights; a third a hammer; and the reſt of the cavalcade are armed with ſticks, and other weapons ne-ceſſary to puniſh offenders.

This groupe is always preceded by ſome perſons in diſguiſe, who take a loaf ſecretly from a ſhop, or the weights and ſcales of a dealer in fruit, or other articles, and every thing which may convict the delinquents of a fraud.

The bread carried to the magiſtrate is placed in the ſcale oppoſite to its juſt weight, whilſt the baker, already ſeized, and in the preſence of his Judge, awaits the decree which is to pronounce him innocent, to order him the baſtinado, or even to in-flict a little ſeverer puniſhment upon him, ſuch as having his ears nailed to his ſhop;

or,

or, in short, hanging him, if the Judge happens to be out of humour. But it is still more remarkable that the real baker, the proprietor of the oven, the fellow whose knavery is punished, has nothing to do in the affair ; he enjoys quietly at his house the daily produce of the false weights which are condemned, and leaves one of his journeymen, the chief manager of his oven, to all the danger, and all the inconveniences of his malverfation. The latter, for double wages, undertakes to perfonate his mafter, and this advantageous fituation is folicited by the fecond journeyman, after the firft is hanged : nobody is difcouraged. It muft however be owned, that thefe punifhments are by no means fo frequent, as they are frequently merited.

The compofition paid by the mafter bakers to the Stambol Effendiffy is confiderable ; and if this magiftrate is obliged to prevent great abufes, and palpable frauds, he has a very material intereft likewife in overlooking many impofitions in this trade, to obtain the tribute which they pay him ; but he has no regard whatever for the fmall dealers, who go about the ftreets ; their weights and fcales are feized and broken in

pieces

pieces with a hammer for the flighteft deficiency, and this ceremony is ufually terminated by the baftinado, unlefs thefe unfortunate people know how to extricate themfelves after the Turkifh manner.—The moft
dexterous accommodate the matter, even
before it comes within the cognizance of
the Judge, and buy themfelves off at a
cheaper rate from the guards in difguife, by
whom they have been apprehended, and
who in their turn, convert their little employment too to profit.

Befides thefe precautions for afcertaining
fairnefs in the fale of provifions, the government fixes their price; but one pays,
notwithftanding, the full value for every
thing. Under defpotifm the multitude is
daily duped. The people do not expect a
comfortable living; they are not accuftomed to that ftate; but they are fometimes
feized with fits of grief and defpair. On
thefe occafions they affume the tone and
character of their fuperiors; they will be
obeyed, and imagine they are fo, when, to
remedy the complaints extorted from them
by the dearnefs of living, the Vifir orders
provifions to be fold at a lower price, and
that going out *incognito* during the publication

tion of this law, the Minister makes them hang up a baker's boy ; nobody inquires into the justice of the pretext, the miserable wretch is sacrificed ; but every body finds the bread a great deal better.

How can so sovereign a contempt for human nature amongst the Turks consist with that whimsical beneficence they display towards certain animals the most useless to society ? Barbarity itself, no doubt, stands in need of some relaxation ; whilst it crushes mankind under the weight of its iron sceptre, it condescends to smile on objects whose insignificance give no occasion for alarm ; and the pride of the despot blending all beings together in one common contempt, selects its favourites from amongst the weakest.

It is doubtless on this principle that the government, whilst it exercises the most rigorous monopoly of corn for the consumption of the capital, by an extraction ruinous to the husbandman, and a distribution less burthensome to the baker than to the consumer, grants so much per cent. in favour of the turtle doves. A cloud of these birds continually fall upon the loaded boats which traverse the harbour of Constantinople,

ftantinople, and carry the corn, uncovered,
either to the ftore-houfes, or the mills, without the boatmen attempting to put a ftop
to their voracioufnefs. The eafe with which
they are permitted to glean the corn, attracts
them in fuch flocks, that I have feen them
perched on the rowers fhoulders, waiting
in their turns for a vacant place to fill their
crops.

It is from very fhallow obfervations alfo
that travellers have extolled the charity of
the Turks towards other animals.

There is in Conftantinople a great number of dogs of the fame kind as the fhepherd's dog, that is to fay, with fox's ears
and muzzles. Thefe animals, difperfed
through every quarter of the town, feem
to have the fame origin ; but they belong
to no particular mafters, and the dogs of
each diftrict make a common caufe againft
fuch marauders as encroach upon their limits. It is eafy, from their haggard looks,
their feeble and languid fteps, as well as
their exceflive lanknefs, to diftinguifh fuch
of them as not having been born in the
quarter of the fhambles, are reduced to live
on the excrement thrown into the ftreets,
and for which they are fortunately indebted

to

to the bad adminiftration of the police. The prodigality of the children, whom they are very affiduous in careffing, procures them alfo fome refource. The females of this needy clafs, fometimes obtain the end of a mat, between two pofts, to fuckle their young on; but notwithftanding thefe trifling fuccours, all thofe at a diftance from the town fhambles, do very little honour to the Turkifh charity. Always miferable, always more or lefs confumptive, and often lame, they feem to offer a ftanding reproach to thofe travellers who have celebrated the charms and comforts of their exiftence *.

Travellers have likewife celebrated as a good work the Turkifh cuftom of feeding their cats with fheeps livers, faid to be diftributed to thofe animals by pious perfons, who devote themfelves to this holy action. This would not, in fact, be either more foolifh, or more fingular, than the ftory of the doves; but one fact does not prove the other, and every thing connected with man-

* In this defcription we fee nothing like that race of dogs we call Turkifh dogs, which are no more known in Turkey than our Turkifh beds, Turkifh robes, and the reft of thofe novelties on which we are pleafed to beftow that name.

ners,

ners, merits a circumstantial and well di-
gested discussion.

The Turks, as well as the Jews, have
their prohibited food; their law obliges
them to bleed and wash what they eat; it
prohibits them also the use of certain parts
of the animal, such as the liver, the lungs,
&c. The butchers must provide, therefore,
for the sale of such articles as suit only the
Christians.

Dgiherdgis, (sellers of liver) carrying a
long stick on their shoulders on which hang
their goods, announce them for sale by
bawling out; but never bestow them gratis.
The quantity of sheep daily slaughtered in
an immense city, where less beef is eaten,
which the Turks are not so fond of, necessarily multiplies these sellers of liver, who
daily take their rounds to dispose of them
in wholesale to the Christians, who eat them,
and in retail to the old women, who in
every country are fond of cats, without being more charitable towards them; but idle-
ness, which is constantly searching after
amusement, furnishes these Dgiherdgis with
another very abundant sale.

The manner of existence of a Turk, who
is so much at his ease as to have nothing to

L 5   do,

do, is to go every day from his own houfe,
feat himfelf in preference in a fhop where
fmoaking tobacco is fold. There, under
pretence of trying to find fome new quality
in that article, he fmokes feveral pipes without paying, and enjoys over and above, the
view of the paffengers, who, on their part,
amufe themfelves with the indolent gravity
of the Turks, and the refpectful appearance
of two or three footmen, who ftand by his
fide with their hands croffed on their waifts.
In this pofition, the firft liver feller who
paffes, ftops, and boafts his talent of affembling all the cats of the diftrict, fays a
few good things to divert his excellency,
and obtains permiffion to begin his operations. The paffengers ftop, the cats affemble
in the twinkling of an eye, at the watch
word; the dealer's fhoulders are covered
with them, and they hang to his cloaths :
he quickly furnifhes his troublefome guefts
with a repaft; the confequential gentleman
who is amufed by this fcene, pays the fellow ; and the European, either ignorant of
the language or little acquainted with it,
and who does not live enough amongft the
Turks to ftudy their genius, and their manners, thinks he has feen an act of charity,
                                    publifhes

publifhes it as fuch without further inquiry, and thus gives fanction to an error.

Mankind ftand fo much in need of mutual affiftance, that the focial virtues ought undoubtedly to be more familiar to them than they generally are. Thefe virtues feem to offer a natural remedy againft thofe misfortunes and neceflities which are common to us all; and, from this confideration, ought to be practifed with more zeal and efficacy amongft an oppreffed people; but defpotifm deftroys every fentiment of humanity and commifferation in the victims whom it hourly facrifices: deftitute itfelf of thofe feelings, it only infpires men, groaning under the weight of its oppreffion, with the defire of becoming oppreffors. Tyranny owes all its flaves to the defire of tyrannizing over others; and perfecution is fo natural in Turkey, that there actually exifts a formal compact in the country, a mutual agreement not to hurt each other.

A Turk who had been Couchedghy-Bachi *, under the reign of the three favourites of Sultan Mahomout, whom he was obliged to facrifice, and of whom I have already

* Couchedghy-Bachi ; the Lieutenant of the Boftandgy Bachi.

fpoken

ſpoken at the beginning of theſe Memoirs, was very intimate with my father-in-law. The government ſtill made uſe of his un- derſtanding and his talents in their ſecret inquiries. Buſineſs of this nature had brought him to Pera *. He was deſirous of becoming acquainted with me; and ſeem- ing to regret that his affairs did not permit him to make a longer ſtay, he took leave, promiſing to return in a ſhort time. Al- ready I had conducted him half way down ſtairs, when ſtopping ſuddenly, and turning round ſhort to one of my people, " Bring " me quickly," ſays he, " ſome bread and " ſalt." I was as much ſurprized at this whimſical requeſt, as at the earneſtneſs with which the ſervant flew to ſatisfy him. What he aſked for is brought him; he takes a little ſalt between his finger and thumb, with a myſterious air, and puts it on his bread,

* Pera, a ſuburb where the Ambaſſadors, and al- moſt all the foreign merchants reſide, except the French, who in general live together at Galata. But it muſt not be imagined that theſe two quarters are appropriated excluſively to the Europeans. The Turks, the Greeks, the Jews, and the Armenians, who inhabit them, amount to more than fifty thou- ſand ſouls, to whom are joined two or three hundred real or pretended Europeans.

which

which he eats with a religious gravity, and takes his leave, assuring me that thenceforward I might depend upon him. I obtained an explanation of every thing important and significant in this ceremony *. We shall see, however, that this very man, becoming Visir, under the name of Moldovandgi Pacha, was at least tempted to violate his oath with respect to me. However that may be, if this sort of oath be not always religiously observed, it serves pretty often as a check to moderate that spirit of revenge to which the Turks are so naturally addicted. Their rage seldom shews itself in the first heat of passion ; they never fight duels ; but they assassinate ; and it is thus they decide all quarrels which never can be reconciled. The person offended publicly whets his knife, or prepares his fire-arms ; some friends strive to appease him, whilst others excite and encourage him to the murder ; but no measures are used tending to prevent the crime which these preparatives proclaim. Drunkenness, however, must precede it. The Turk is obliged to find in

* The Turks hold it to be the highest ingratitude to forget those who have given them food, which is represented by the bread and salt in this ceremony.

wine,

wine, the degree of courage neceffary to fupply his anger. Arrived at this pitch, he leaves the tavern, and there is no longer any fafety for the offender, except in the want of fkill of the offended perfon. If the murder be committed, and the guard, who are armed only with fticks *, purfue the affaffin, it is then that he exhibits real proofs of courage ; he defends himfelf like a lion ; one would imagine that the crime had elevated his foul ; and if he at length fubmits, the threats of his affociates very foon bring the relations of the deceafed to a compofition, which leaves the guilty in poffeffion of

* The patroles who go through the city to preferve order, and for the public fafety, are only armed with fticks, in the fhape of little clubs, the thick end of which is dipped in rofin. When a criminal avails himfelf of his activity to efcape, he is foon overturned by the addrefs of the guards, who throw their fticks at his legs. One very often fees people thrown down in this manner, who are no otherwife culpable than by going too quick about their bufinefs. It is a little amufement by which the guards exercife their talent for laying hold of criminals; but when thefe latter have fire arms, the guards are more careful to avoid meeting, than ardent in the purfuit of them.

that

that high efteem which this event infures
him †.

It is only a few hired Turks, fome Chriftians, or Jews, who furnifh examples of
public punifhments for the murders they
may commit. In this cafe the criminal,
conducted to the Porte, there receives his
fentence. No apparatus accompanies his
execution; and I have met fome of them
paffing through the croud, with which the
ftreets are filled, converfing with the men
who were to be their executioners. The
criminal only has his hands tied, and the
executioner holds him by the waift. This
is the moment to negociate with the relations of the deceafed, and to attempt the ac-
commodation I have mentioned. I have
been affured by fome perfons, that bargains
of this kind fometimes fail from the avarice
of the criminal. The fact appears highly
improbable; but fuppofing it to be true,
it muft arife, no doubt, from this circumftance, that under a defpotic government

† There is no exaggeration in this; they never fay,
but as an eulogium, fuch a one has killed fuch another: he who has killed ten, is the hero of his quarter;
no entertainment without him; his friendfhip is a
fafeguard.

riches

riches are every thing, and life of very little value.

The habit of defpifing the Chriftians, and of honouring the Turks, has eftablifhed the cuftom of placing the criminal's head, if he be a true believer, on his arm, which is bent for the purpofe; and that of an infidel on his pofteriors.

Nothing would be wanting to complete the barbarity of the Turks, but to imitate the cuftom in France, of extending the punifhment of a perfonal crime, fo as to cover with the infamy of his execution, thofe innocent perfons who have the misfortune to be related to the guilty. In Turkey, on the contrary, they infcribe on his grave ftone the name of the deceafed, and the nature of his punifhment; and I knew an European who was very ill received on this account, by a Greek woman of diftinction, whofe hufband had been juft hanged for a court broil. He thought it neceffary to condole with her on this event, and dwelt particularly on the nature of the punifhment. " How do you think he ought to have died then?" exclaimed the woman in rage. " Let me tell you, Sir, that nobody in my family has died like a Raccal *." The European, aftonifhed, withdrew, wifhing all her relations an happy exit. This prejudice, fo very different from ours, is again explained by defpotifm. To be pu- nifhed for a ftate crime, implies that the criminal muft have been of fome import- ance to the ftate. Men fubmit to a ftate of dependance only in the hopes of com- manding in their turn ; this is the origin of flavery ; it feeds the vanity of the flave, and is the only fentiment of honour which can exift under defpotifm.

Although we have already feen that drun- kennefs hurries on the Turks to crimes, and gives them the force neceffary to com- mit them, and although wine be prohibited by the law, the taverns at Conftantinople are as public, and as numerous as public houfes in our towns; the government makes them pay, and protects them. Such of the Turks as frequent them, regularly get drunk ; and the confumption becoming a revenue of the Exchequer, is farmed out to

* Raccal, a grocer; they ufually die in their beds; this is the profeffion which they have the cuftom of contemptuoufly oppofing to the moft diftinguifhed fi- tuations.

an

an Intendant, called Charab Eminy ‡. This officer receives the duties of entry ; but the police of the taverns, as well as the fees they make them pay, belong to the firſt magiſtrate, and to the particular governors of the reſpective quarters.

I have ſaid, that in the ſolemn feaſts, the taverns are ſhut to avoid, during that period, the fatal effects of the habitual debauchery of the people. The police puts a ſeal on the door of every tavern ; but a wicket contrived below, which the police pretends not to ſee, always leaves a free and public entry ; it coſts no more than a ſlight ſtoop of the body to evade the law, and get drunk at pleaſure.

The three days of bairam, however, excite a ſort of anxiety on the part of government to prevent the diſorders which drunkenneſs might occaſion. The Ramazan which precedes theſe holidays, is the Lunar month deſtined to a faſt, and its epocha is advanced annually eleven days. This

‡ Charab Eminy, Intendant of the Wine ; an employment never given by the government but to a Turk ; he is the renter of that part of the grants, and collects the duties either in the quality of farm or direction.

time

time of abftinence, copied by Mahomet from the Chriftian fafts, confifts among the Turks, as it formerly did in the primitive church, in taking no nourifhment whilft the Sun is on the horizon. It is evident that the part of the Lunar revolution, which brings the Ramazan towards the winter folftice, makes it lefs infupportable than that which places it in the fummer folftice, from the length of the days and the exceffive heat which prevails during the time of abftinence; but the working clafs appear alone to fuffer all the rigour of the Ramazan; deprived, during the day, of a glafs of water to quench the thirft, or refrefh the mouth, the fetting fun prefents them only with a frugal repaft, with a little repofe from fatigue, which is again interrupted by prayers, and the neceffity of eating before funrife.

The Ramazan offers a very different picture amongft people of opulence. It is effeminacy, fleeping in the arms of hypocrify, and which only awakens to refign itfelf to the pleafures of good cheer, mufic, and of every thing which can compenfate to fenfuality for the pain of abftinence.

Submiffive

Submiffive to the revolution of a period prefcribed by the laws, and always impatient for its expiration, a Turk, during the Ramazan, is never tired of counting the hours or the minutes; he encompaffes himfelf with all the watches and all the clocks he is mafter of, and this is the period in which Geneva collects the principal part of the tribute her induftry impofes on the Turks. This lucrative commerce would become infinitely more fo, if, by a double quadrature fo difpofed as to fhorten the fpiral of the balance, or gradually to raife the point of fufpenfion of the pendulum, they could advance the movement of the hands, and retard them by inverting the fame operation, relatively to the fetting of the fun, which the Turks always ftate at twelve hours; in this cafe I would engage, that fenfible only to this diurnal refult, they would not perceive that the quicknefs or flownefs of the vibrations, by dividing the difference, would alter the duration of each particular hour.

The moft regular watch in the world, however, would not be fufficient to determine the moment of finifhing the faft; the cryers of the Mofques, placed in the galleries

ries of the minarets, obferve from thence the
fetting of the fun, and the firft fignal muft
be given from that of Saint Sophia, by
chaunting the invitation to prayers, which
the other muezzins repeat from their minarets. At this period the impatience of
the Turks, the moft devout of whom always begin by ablution, leads generally to
the luxury of fmoaking, which is the firft
of their wants.

But if the Turks wait until the fun dif-
appears, to allow themfelves fome nourifhment, they are not lefs attentive to afcertain minutely the beginning of the new
moon, to enter into the Ramazan; and in
general it is only to begin this faft that they
place a full and unlimited confidence in
aftronomical calculations. It is remarked,
in fact, that this moon, dedicated to abftinence, ufually lafts no longer than eight
and twenty days; and that the perfons appointed to obferve this planet, and to make
a formal declaration of it to the Porte, are
always rather late in obferving the firft
gleam of light which marks its renewal;
but in return they are much lefs fcrupulous
in afferting the appearance of the following
moon, which commences the Bairam, and
is

is announced to the public by difcharges of artillery.

The feftival, however, which fucceeds the term of abftinence amongft the Turks, cannot be compared with the folemnity which follows the Chriftian Lent; and one only difcóvers a fort of imitation of the Pafcal Lamb, in the *Courbam Bairam*, the Bairam of the Sacrifice. This fecond Pafcal feaft does not take place until fix weeks after the former. The Grand Signior, all the great men, and every body who can afford it, kill one or more fheep on that day. A proportionable number of thefe animals are particularly taken care of for that purpofe, and have their wool combed and their horns gilt, and the moment of facrificing thefe offerings muft be calculated for the very inftant when the fame facrifice takes place at Mecca.

The epocha of the Bairam is alfo that of the greateft luxuries; every body purchafes, or gives, or receives new cloaths. It is the time, too, for parties of pleafure of every kind, which always produce fome irregularities and difagreeable circumftances on the part of the walkers out, who difperfe themfelves through the different villages

lages for three or four leagues round Conftantinople, and where the Turks, newly
clad, *thoroughly abfolved*, and always well
armed, think that they may perpetrate every
thing with impunity, and exact what they
think proper from the unhappy Greeks who
vegetate in thofe villages.

The aqueducts which convey water to
Conftantinople, are often the object of the
Turkifh walks ; but we may fuppofe that
it is neither to admire the architecture of
thefe buildings, nor to judge of the falu-
brity of the water, that the curious flock
there in crouds.   They take great pains to
carry wine and other things there to regale'
themfelves; they take poffeffion of the ru-
ined kiofks built by the Emperors at the
fame time with the edifices deftined to collect the rain water, and convey it to the
capital.

The aqueducts which the Turks have
been compelled to fubftitute for the ancient
cifterns, are fo badly conftructed, that a
comparifon between them and the aqueduct
of the Greeks, muft give an advantageous
idea of the latter.

The edifice, built in the time of Juftinian, offers nothing interefting either in
point

point of boldnefs, or lightnefs of architecture. The good tafte of the architect is
ftill lefs confpicuous ; he feems only to
have ftudied to deceive the eye in the form
of the pillars, by giving them the appearance of folid maffes in the air, whilft thofe
inverted cones form reliefs, which project
too much at their bafis. A mixture of
large Gothic arches, and of fmall circular
ones, are neither bolder nor more agreeable to the eye ; and I have only looked
upon this ftructure as interefting, in as far
as it may ferve to fix the period at which
good tafte in architecture began to decline
amongft the Greeks.

The aqueducts of the Turks are of a
more determinate kind ; no proportion in
the plan, no choice in the materials, no
fkill or neatnefs in their diftribution ; one
is aftonifhed at the immenfity of the work,
—one is out of patience at its imperfec-
tion ; every thing announces ignorance fet
in motion by force, and kept in pay by
avarice.

Thefe faults are lefs ftriking in the
Mofques built by the Turkifh Emperors
at Conftantinople, becaufe all thefe edifices, built under the eye of the Sultans,

and

and after the model of Saint Sophia, are more or lefs ornamented, and always well taken care of, from motives of fear and vanity, by the Greeks or Armenians, who are the undertakers of them. There are even fome Mofques *, which, built on the plan of that ancient Greek church, have furpaffed their model; but the model is very far from being a mafter-piece; and one would prefume, that a more attentive examination might have prevented travellers from lavifhing their praifes on the ftructure of Saint Sophia. Had thefe travellers been more fkilled in architecture, they might have concluded, from the difplacing of the pillars alone, that after having œconomifed in the original plan, the maffes neceffary for folidity, they have been unreafonably lavifh in the fpurs with which the building is at length fupported, they might have feen too, by meafuring with the eye, the arch of the exterior dome, that the flat roof which ferves for cieling, offers only an illufory boldnefs,

* The Mofque of Sultan Achmet, and that of Checkzade, are of a more flender conftruction; and the former ornamented with fix Minarets, extends the whole place of the Hyppodromos.

and that far from fupporting itfelf, independant of the building, it is fufpended by
the full centre which covers it. I have
been affured even, that this inner dome
was built of pumice ftone, bound with a
very fine cement of pafte and lime, which
reduces to nothing this pretended wonder.
The infide decoration does no greater honour to the age of Conftantine †. A great
quantity of columns fet it at different diftances, without proportion, the module of
which appears to have been miftaken in
their height, in their bafes, and in their
capitals; no order in the entablature, no
rule, no tafte in the profiles, thefe furely
do not merit fo much celebrity. There is
nothing in fact to admire in that building,
but the richnefs and abundance of materials, in which one would be tempted to
imagine one difcovered thofe precious ruins,

---

† It is pretended, that this edifice, built by Conftantine, and deftroyed by an earthquake, was rebuilt
by Juftinian; but I think we fhould only attribute to
this laft emperor, the maffes of ftone by way of fpurs
erected on the outfide to fupport the pillars, which
had given way in confequence of the earthquake.
The effect of thefe fhocks is ftill apparent from the
inclination of the columns, whofe bafis of bronze do
not equally fupport them.

which

which are no longer to be found at Delphi or at Delos.

But the beauty of the Mosaics which adorned the roof of Saint Sophia is indisputable: I have been still able to discover the end of the wings of the four cherubins, which were supported by the cornice, at the spring of the arch of the four pillars. The obstinacy of the Turks in daubing this dome with lime water, leaves nothing to be seen at this day of these Mosaics, and they are daily compleating their destruction, by continuing to tear off splinters, which a barbarous curiosity purchases of that ignorance and avidity which as barbarously destroys them.

Some pieces of these Mosaics, split into crystals of three or four cubic lines, being sent to Vienna to be cut, produced stone of different colours of a very fine lustre, and great hardness.

The contempt of the Turks for the most precious work we know of, leaves no doubt of the simplicity of the ornaments which decorate their other Mosques. These ornaments consist in no more than four large tables, on which are written the names of the four disciples of Mahomet;

several

several passages of the Coran are also written in different places, and particularly towards the pulpit, from whence this sacred book is read during the meditation which precedes the prayer. I must add, that the women admitted also into the Mosques, place themselves only in the part destined to their use; and if the Turkish manners had not rendered that separation necessary in other respects, one would pardon their establishing it in their temples, where order and silence ought constantly to remind us, that if the necessities of life have limited and regulated certain intervals in divine worship, we cannot offer too respectful an adoration in the temple consecrated to the Eternal Being.

Vocal music, instead of the noise of bells, announces the hour of prayer, in an Arabic formula, which combines the unity of God, the mission of the Prophet, prayers and good works. The muezzins of each Mosque * mount for that purpose on their minarets. This sort of steeple,

---

* Muezzins,—Cryers of the Mosque; it is an office which the Iman performs himself in the smaller benefices, but in the great Mosques it is a distinct office.

which

which refemble columns, are fmall hollow
towers of four or five feet diameter; they
rife of an equal thicknefs from the angles
of the Mofque, to the height of the domes,
where a projecting gallery of twenty or
thirty inches, communicates with a wind-
ing ftair-cafe, which leads to it by a little
gate, always facing Mecca. The mina-
ret then diminifhing about a fourth of its
thicknefs, continues to rife about a fifth
or fixth part of its height; and terminates
in a pointed cone, covered with lead, and
finifhed in a fort of crefcent, the two ex-
tremities of which, in a fluted curve, and
very near each other, ufually encircle the
name of God, cut out of the metal. The
principal Mofques have feveral of thefe
minarets, to each of which the galleries
are doubled or trebled; but thofe of Saint
Sophia have only one; they are alfo the
leaft lofty, and the leaft flender †.

It might be proper, doubtlefs, in this
place, to afcertain the eftimation in which
the Turks hold the crefcent; but I fhall

† Thefe minarets, which were doubtlefs built foon
after the taking of Conftantinople, are become difagreeable to the eye, from the lightnefs and boldnefs
of thofe which have been fince conftructed.

have

have occasion to treat of this matter in speaking of the Grand Signior's artillery; and I shall confine myself at present to observe, that in rebuilding the Visir's palace, after the fire I have spoken of, the architect made use of fleurs de lys, with four leaves, for the last ornament of the cupola covering the gate which separates the two courts. He substituted this ornament for the crescents which were on the former gate. Observing this little decoration at the Palace of France, he adopted it, and nobody imagined that it had any meaning.

From a refinement of the same nature, but of a very different effect, two antique green columns, placed by way of ornament at the principal gate of the Seraglio, are supported on their capitals. I complained of this to the superintendant of the buildings, who very judiciously observed to me, that the foliage of the capitals, so ingeniously carved, richly merited to be placed within the reach of admiration.

Constantinople, on the side of the sea, furnishes likewise the most painful prospect: one sees there a forest of columns, ranged cross-ways, and on several beds,
which

which ferve as a foundation for her lofty walls; and the richeft ruins, confounded with the vileft materials, prefent, at every ftep, the afflicting picture of ignorance and barbarifm, confufedly jumbled with the precious remains of the ancient Grecian knowledge.

To finifh this painting of the Turks, and to give an idea of their ftupid pride, it will be fufficient to cite one of their favourite adages:

Riches in India,
Wit in Europe,
and
Pomp amongft the Ottomans.

The picture of the Grand Signior's proceffion on the day of Coronation, has given an idea of their fo much boafted pomp; but I muft allow that there is fomething brilliant and ftriking enough in the cavalcade which accompanies the Grand Signior when he goes out upon the fea. The grace, the lightnefs, the richnefs of his boats, can be compared with nothing of that kind we have amongft us. His Highnefs alone has the right of having a tilt covered with fcarlet, and crowned with three gilded lanterns, and twenty-fix rowers;

ers; a fimilar boat which follows for any occafion that may offer, always ferves him to return in. The different officers of the Court attend him, each in the boats appropriated to them ; and their great number, joined to the precifion of the ftrokes of the oars, and the quicknefs of the motion, prefents the moft majeftic profpect, and the moft agreeable coup d'œil.

When the Grand Signior's fon is of age to appear in public, his boat, rowed alfo by fix and twenty rowers, is diftinguifhed by a blue tilt, after which the Vifir is the only perfon who can have a tilt ; but it muft be green, and his boat muft not have more than twenty-four rowers.

The Mufti, expofed in his boat to the intemperance of the air, like the loweft individual, is only diftinguifhed by nine pair of oars, and the privilege of having two men on each bench.

The boats of the other great men, whofe number of oars is determined alfo by the importance of their offices, have only one rower on each bench, as well as the foreign Ambaffadors, who likewife have no right to carry a tilt.

But

But the boats of the harem, which carry the Grand Signior's wives, are manned with twenty-four rowers, and have white co-vered tilts, ſhut alternately by Venetian blinds; walls of canvaſs are prepared like-wiſe for their reception, of which a little, narrow ſtreet is formed, which runs from the gate of the Seraglio to the boats. When they go out to walk, which is very ſeldom, the rural harem which is prepared for them, is ſurrounded likewiſe in the ſame manner, and they are introduced into it with the ſame precaution. Black eunuchs ſurround this incloſure, and Aſſequis *, armed with carbines, form a ſecond line of circum-vallation to defend the approaches. Un-fortunate the man, who, ignorant of theſe diſpoſitions, comes within gun ſhot! The ſtroke of death would be his firſt warning. It is thus that the wives of the Prince, kept always in a fold like ſheep, enjoy the pleaſure of breathing the freſh air.

This extraordinary entertainment gives, undoubtedly no very exalted idea of the perpetual joys which reign in the harem

---

* Boſtandgi Aſſequis, who perform the office of the Prevote de L'hotel in France; they are the grenadiers of the corps of Boſtandgis.

of the Grand Signior. One may conceive that the women exiſt there leſs agreeably, than in this little park, ſince it is intended as a party of pleaſure. Here is matter enough, no doubt, to reform many miſtaken ideas.

Thoſe which I had at firſt collected of the Turkiſh government and military were incorrect. One can only judge of men in action; and I reſerve thoſe particulars for the events of the laſt war, which developed them more completely to me. Theſe hiſtorical details will bring me back to Conſtantinople, from whence I ſet out in 1763, on my return to France, to acquaint the Miniſtry that I was loſing my time, and the King his money, were I not to be more uſefully employed.

END OF THE FIRST VOLUME.